Also by Joy Williams

# HARROW

# HARROW

*A novel*

## Joy Williams

Alfred A. Knopf, New York

2021

THIS IS A BORZOI BOOK
PUBLISHED BY ALFRED A. KNOPF

Library of Congress Cataloging-in-Publication Data
Names: Williams, Joy, 1944– author.
Title: Harrow: a novel / Joy Williams.
Description: First Edition. | New York: Alfred A. Knopf, 2021.
Identifiers: LCCN 2020050338 (print) | LCCN 2020050339 (ebook) |
ISBN 9780525657569 (hardcover) | ISBN 9780525657576 (ebook)
Subjects: GSAFD: Fantasy fiction.
Classification: LCC PS3573.I4496 H37 2021 (print) |
LCC PS3573.I4496 (ebook) | DDC 813/.54—dc23
LC record available at https://lccn.loc.gov/2020050338
LC ebook record available at https://lccn.loc.gov/2020050339

Jacket image: (horse) Mary Evans Picture Library
Jacket design by Kelly Blair

Manufactured in the United States of America
First Edition

For JZ

On the vehicle that transported them was written: *All creatures of whatever description, named or unnamed, are to be brought with us on the Great Journey*. It was a perfect assurance becoming increasingly illegible. They believed themselves to be tourists. They wore sun hats and clutched sippy cups. Oh! they'd exclaim.

The rocks were pretty in a certain light.

The air was pleasant.

Was it not Socrates who doubted that a person was a human being at birth? He did so doubt. Those were the days when a human being was something to be aspired to.

They didn't want to be told, shown maybe. Each felt the others to be as inanimate as dolls. They appreciated the paradox of being together in this but not really.

In the distance, something wheeled slowly in the air.

The beyond is in *this* life, a pretty exciting notion.

They paid scant attention to the scrimshawed vehicle that transported them. That was the skin outside them. It was lost on them really. The skein of ice on mud held patterns too.

Something fled in its shadow before them.

They had come from other places and the inevitable comparisons and confidences arose. They missed different things. They thought they'd see those things again here.

Where are the antelopes with their lovely masks . . . Where are the milty streams . . .

No one had brought a pen or a camera or a tin of paints.

I left my paints behind. Could hardly do this justice, I thought.

Yes. Look at these canyon walls.

When I first heard a cave breathe? I'll tell you, I was scared. Something like that breathing. Inhale, exhale. The holes just scream.

Excuse me, we weren't talking caves, we were talking canyons.

When my daddy had his cerebral hemorrhage he couldn't talk no more but he could scream and sing.

That's the left. When it affects the left.

Will this way go? That's canyoneering jargon. When they say, *I don't know if this way will go,* they mean . . .

I just got back from the desert, the American one of course, was visiting my nephew, my sister's boy. He's got himself an eagle now. He'll kill anything to support that eagle.

How did he come by that?

Lottery. Now he's got to support it which means feeding it. He shoots all manner of things for it but he's got a connection at the grocery store who gives him stuff, too, mostly ham. Have you ever seen anything stiller than a ham? I've certainly not. You'd think an eagle wouldn't care for anything that still.

What else did you do in the desert, Danielle?

Nothing stiller than a ham. That's funny.

I don't believe I'd care for the desert. You'd have to look at it, there'd be no choice. What else would there be to look at.

Well they're putting in lots of solar grids now. They're paving the desert floor with panels. Some poor devil whose job it is to have to look at those. They're like the sheepherders of yore living in these peanut trailers, farming the sun and the wind. But the wind's dying down out there, more and more no wind days a month. Isn't that the darndest thing? It's like the wind is saying I WILL NOT BE ENSLAVED.

Danielle, you are a riot today.

I think the world is dying because we were dead to its astonishments pretty much. It'll be around but it will become less and less until it's finally compatible with our feelings for it.

You are not our guide. You shouldn't talk like you're our guide.

I do like some of the guides better than others.

Some of them are nicer.

Death's angels. They're death's angels, the nicer ones.

I'd like to go back to the little rooms now. Aren't there still the little rooms where we can be?

Oh what have we done!! someone cried.

BOOK ONE

If they do this when the wood is green,
What will happen when the wood is dry?

—LUKE 23:31

My MOTHER AND FATHER NAMED ME LAMB. MY MOTHER BE-
lieved that I had died as an infant but had then come back to the
life we shared. As I grew, her intention and need was to put me
in touch with where I had been when I was dead, what I remem-
bered of it and what I had learned. She believed I was destined for
something extraordinary.

My father did not believe I had ever been dead. Nor did any of
the doctors they consulted.

A young man was watching me the night I was said to have
died. He did not harm me was the truth of it. It was just a story
that was to grow up around us both, causing us both to be outcasts.

My mother and father were at a dance, the first dance of the
summer.

My mother lacked good judgment in many things. She would
be the first to admit it. She had taken up with this young man who
was still a teenager a little more than a month after I was born.
He was a town boy, he delivered our groceries and was Catho-
lic as well. His mother made him go to St. Margaret's but to my
mother he railed against the constraints of the church. She found
him sweet—his sometimes impotence, his muscles, his dark, dark
hair, his inchoate manner of thinking . . . sweet.

She enjoyed having him explain Purgatory to her.

"They abolished it," he said.

"How utterly ridiculous. I just don't think they can do that, do you?"

"They did, but it still exists."

"And one should fear it but one should guard against excessive fear. One mustn't feel overwhelmed. One must always keep in mind that justice punishes and mercy pardons." She looked at him somberly.

"Correct."

"And tell me again how long a person of faith would have to spend there, assuming that even being very good this person would still manage to commit ten wrongs a day. Which is a conservative number by any reckoning."

A priest had told his mother that each wrong results in one hour of Purgatory. Even if you strive tirelessly to be good you'll be racking up faults by the thousands and will meet God dangerously in debt, the priest, a geriatric traditionalist, said. After fifty years, say, you've accumulated 150,000 faults and got rid of half of them through penance and good works but you'd still have 75,000 hours to pay down. And that would take seven years, ten months and fifteen days.

"I've told you what my mother was told," he said. "You're just fucking with me."

"I just love the calculations. They're so precise."

"They abolished it, but that doesn't mean we're relieved of the necessity of going there."

Yes, my mother found him sweet. His smooth face and square hands, the practiced roll of his walk, his threadbare jeans, the impracticality and poverty of his life. She arranged to have him babysit when she and my father went to the first club function of the new season. It amused her to hire her unlikely lover in this manner and bring him into the very heart of our home.

From birth I had been remarkably serene and considerate, seldom crying and sleeping straight through the night, so the likeli-

hood was small that this directionless young man would have to have any interaction with me at all. If I cried he was to call them at the club.

The dance floor was laid out on the sand. It was Mexican Night, Fiesta Night in Olde New England. The following week it would be Argentine/Tango Night. Modest fireworks were being set off. A ragged hiss, then a streaming downward, the light enfolded by the waves. Small boats rocked gently on their moorings.

"There are some Mexicans, in Chiapas, I think, who believe the world's a cube," the man who would be commodore said.

"I want the tequila that's got the scorpion in the bottle," my mother said, laughing, and the people at their table laughed, too, for *it's a worm, Martha, a worm . . .*

She laughed, "I hate my name so much."

"But you've given your baby such an interesting name," her friend Slim teased.

"That's not her legal name of course," my father said. "It's just for now. Her name is Christen."

"Oh him and his damn boats," my mother said. "Everything has to be connected to boats. I've insisted on the letter *K* at least."

"Let's get a little dinghy," a man on my mother's left said. He was new, she didn't know who he was.

"What a pretty charm bracelet," the banker's wife said. Her husband was a loan officer, recently promoted.

"You must be happy," someone said, congratulating him. "We am," he said. He firmly believed he wasn't drunk yet but that if he went to the bathroom, which he ached to do, he would be. He knew himself.

"Thank you," Martha said, touching a charm. "This is a new one. It's the zodiacal sign of the Gemini."

"But you didn't have twins, Martha, did you?"

"No, no," she laughed. She hated her laugh. "But that's her sign. She was born in May. On a Thursday."

"Astrology can be fun, I guess," the banker's wife said.

"Fiesta!!" a young man shouted. He was wearing red pants, a tie as a belt and a white shirt on which he'd already spilled bean dip. "Throw down your burdens of time and reason!"

My mother's young man went into the kitchen and put a pot of water on to boil for a package of pasta he'd found in the cupboard. He was always hungry but didn't like people seeing him eat. He found eating tactless.

My mother liked candles, they were all over the house. Some were expensive, but there were others she'd bought in supermarkets as a joke, the wax poured into tall glasses with decals wrapped around them.

St. Martin de Porres with the broom and the cat and the dog and people lying behind him in beds, not looking good. Or the Guardian Angel one, with a winged woman following two barefoot children over a wooden bridge slung over a chasm and clearly unsafe and what were they doing out there by themselves anyway? The prayers on the back of the glass were in Spanish and English and even the most casual examination showed them to be evasive and nonsensical in the extreme. Most of them had cheap wicks and didn't even light or if they did the flame soon drowned in its own wax.

My mother was teasing him, even mocking him, he knew that—his troubled, angry faith, its outrageous sentimentalities and brutal corrections. If it were up to him, he'd told her once, he'd be a Jew, a Zealot in the time of the Roman Empire. They were audacious and went far beyond the norms of consensual behavior. They ripped things apart. They went after Rome and just chewed it to pieces. But then they screwed up, burning the food supplies of their own people during a long siege of Jerusalem in order to force God's hand to act against their enemies. They

figured God would have no choice but to intervene to preserve them, His adherents. But God did nothing and everybody in Jerusalem starved to death.

But to be a Jew your mother had to be a Jewess and his mother was no Jewess. She was a sun-wrinkled dope-fogged ex-hippie whose highest ambition in life was to have someone give her an old Mercedes diesel that she could run on waste fry oil from the restaurant where she worked. Ma, he'd say, it's a seasonal restaurant, it closes the first week of November. How you going to get around after that? You're not thinking, Ma.

He wandered through our house, lighting candles and turning off lights. He came into the nursery and looked at the two framed photographs of my mother that hung on the wall. She was in a bikini, showing off her big belly and wearing the charm bracelet she always wore, glinting with the codes of her known life. The photographs were in black and white, one frontal and the other taken from the side which made her, and what she was carrying, look like suspects in an atypical police lineup.

He looked down into the crib at the baby, me, and I gazed back at him. My name escaped him. He was nothing to me, of course— this figure, this presence, this filament of darkness—but his was the world I would inherit. He said no word to acknowledge or comfort me but sat down in the chair my mother rocked me in in the early mornings before the day began.

I felt his presence disappear then. Then of myself as well, I became no longer aware. I was neither awake nor asleep, nor could I know what was expected of me, for surely something would be expected?

My mother and father were preparing to leave the club. On the drive home my mother felt chilled and wanted my father's jacket to put over her shoulders but he refused. They were already out

of love even then. He turned onto our lane, ignoring her as she theatrically pretended she was freezing. Blackberry bushes and wild roses and Queen Anne's lace lined the road. Every year, they and their few neighbors fought to keep it paved, but the councilmen, *elected* officials, he was forever reminding them, wanted it tarred. The whole matter would end up in court one of these days he feared. They probably would have to get together and hire a lawyer just to protect the false pastoral quality of the road. He said, "Did the power go off?"

The house was lit up like an altar with what must have been every candle my mother possessed. They'd gotten home earlier than they'd intended. Maybe he was entertaining a girl in there, my mother thought, amused.

My parents had misplaced their keys.

"What are you, drunk!" my father demanded when the young man finally appeared at the door. Candles were guttering everywhere and a two-hundred-dollar pot was seared and ruined on the stove. Yet no explanation or apology appeared forthcoming.

Never apologizing or explaining was how the men and boys of the club navigated their days, but such posturing by this presence infuriated my father.

"What are you, drunk!" my father demanded again, puzzled, aware that it was he and my mother who were half-cut from Fiesta Night.

My mother confessed to me that she had giggled—her irate husband, her absurd lover—it was all so preposterous—but she hurried into the nursery and with care picked me up.

"Thomas!" she screamed. "The baby's not breathing."

And then, as she told me, after an eternity, my father appeared and seized me from her arms. When she, in turn, tore me from his grasp, I cried out as I had at birth. And it was, my mother said, as if I were being born all over again.

My father had no more patience for my mother. In the time that was left for them, in the time they remained together, she never stopped wanting another baby, an extra one was perhaps her thinking, a replacement one were I to die again and not return.

"Lion," my mother begged. "We can name him Lion if he's a boy. We can name her Lion if she's a girl."

But my father ignored her. He spent less and less time in our pleasant house and more at the boatyard he managed. He even began designing his own boats, though he suspected that few people would still be sailing for pleasure in the future. The waterways were being increasingly compromised. The demand was for mammoth houseboats with fireplaces and hot tubs. He was disgusted with these vessels and the people who craved them. Still, he continued to refit and repair them. More and more he realized it was best not to try and change the minds of others, best not to resent or struggle. Even the road he had so recently loved, the sandy roller-coaster road leading to our house and beyond which he had sought so to preserve, he was going to let the neighbors have. Soon he would not live there anymore.

My mother's eager beauty faded, her reckless teasing ways. She became more and more convinced that I had died that night and had witnessed ruthless and troubling mysteries which it was essential for me to recall. I had experienced a great reversal and my life, or whatever it was that had been restored to me, must be subject to the most delicate and definitive interpretation. The fact that I was an awkward yet trusting and thoughtful child with few apparent gifts made my presence all the more properly intriguing in my mother's eyes. For were there not many stories of servants or otherwise utterly uncharismatic and unassuming persons turning out to be the enlightened ones who could lead

others out of their lifeless lives and into a new contract with the world?

During my childhood my mother took me to many doctors, all of whom maintained I was perfectly healthy. She was told again and again that she had been mistaken, that if I had stopped breathing for as long as she claimed, any number of neurological issues would have arisen. And they had not. In a crisis of fright, time had played a trick on her, a new and inexperienced mother. Most likely I had never stopped breathing at all.

Yet, my mother was convinced that I had been *somewhere*, in some frightful chaos of non-being that nevertheless contained an observable yet incomprehensible future to which we would all be subjected.

My father moved out, into a suite of rooms above the boat-yard offices. My mother and I continued to live in the seaside house which she neglected. She no longer went to the club or saw her friends, who felt they'd endured quite enough of us and the rumors of that night.

I continued to be subjected to medical examinations and psychological testing. One specialist was interested in me for a time because he believed that only genetic mutations could rewire the brain to cope with the environmental and moral challenges of a ruined, overpopulated world. But he found nothing. He had never found anything. He admitted it was just a sensible, attractive theory.

I remember the results of my last test, the last because my mother no longer had the money to continue. She could not pay— the secular bastards, she called them—and they never contacted us again. She came to believe that our every thought and emotion was being graphed by a newly sinister camarilla. The only way she could save me from this situation was if she severed herself from me. But this belief came later. Until then, I had a ragged succes-

sion of tutors and my mother watched me anxiously, fearful that the error of my return would be corrected.

There were several instances when death could have escorted me once more into the robing room from which I doubted it would have allowed me to emerge again. The one I recall most vividly occurred at the hardware store where my mother had taken me to select a new color for the walls of my bedroom which were still covered with the insipid pink of my infancy. I chose a color called Passing Cloud, and a can of paint mixed by computer to the specifications of that hue spun out of the unsecured door of the machine that was mixing it and soared across the room. Clutching a fistful of paint cards, I could have been brained but was not.

The can of paint, Passing Cloud, a color eventually not chosen for the walls of my room, rolled through the store back to screen repair and slammed into a cardboard box where a pelican awaited pickup by the Bird Lady. There was no sound from the box. The pelican had been found, far north of its normal range, wandering disoriented in the parking lot. Everyone in town had heard about the Bird Lady but we children didn't get taken out to see her much. People applauded her efforts but they found her ten damp acres rescued through donations from becoming another sewer meadow just not that educational. How many times must the children be informed as to how clean the vultures keep their cages, they asked? And the volunteers are so gloomy and the desperate need for lumber and wire, seed, fish and towels never ends . . . I went there once, I cannot remember the circumstances. I found myself in an area where visitors were not supposed to go and there I saw an old oil drum, brimming with amputated wings. I did not speak of this to my mother.

My mother and I became reclusive, increasingly so after an incident which pained both of us to recall. Her former best friend, Slim, had lost her child, a boy of nine. Slim had had difficulty

conceiving but then she did and the boy was extremely bright and quite frail. But then there was something about him breaking his arm, they'd never found out how exactly, and then getting a staph infection in the very wing of the hospital her family had founded, the very hospital in which my father would later lie.

My mother had been attempting to acquaint herself with Buddhism in her continuing quest for guidance in this life. Unfortunately, her first and possibly last attempt to incorporate Zen's playful koans in her interaction with others was with bereaved Slim one bright and windy morning on the beach. It was not even noon but poor Slim was well toasted, her skin and hair reeking of whiskey, her coat incorrectly buttoned. She tearfully recounted the death of her little boy and the travails of her family, everyone hating and blaming everyone now, it was a nightmare, day after day. God knows what possessed my mother to relate one of those annoying Zen stories in an attempt to console her.

"One day, a flock of wild geese was seen flying and the master asked, 'What are they?'" my mother said, gesturing at the empty sky.

"Say?" Slim said.

"'They are wild geese,' the novitiate answered."

"What novitiate?" Slim cried.

"'Whither are they flying?'" my mother continued serenely.

"What the fuck, Martha."

"'They have flown away,' the little monk said."

"What little monk!" Slim's face had become even more flushed.

"And the master, the wise man, said, 'You say they have flown away but all the same they have been here from the very beginning.'"

My mother later admitted that the story was not as engaging as she remembered, but she was nonetheless startled by her friend's reaction.

"You are such a cold cunt, Martha!" Slim said. "All that while you were going on about your child's dying and coming back, boring everyone into a stupor, though we were all so supportive, we carried you for so long listening to your crap and it hadn't even happened and here's my little boy gone forever and you can't even bother to say anything decent. Fuck your little monks and geese, Martha. Fuck you."

And she had stumbled down the beach in a rage, trailing clouds of whiskey fumes.

After that we seldom left the house. My mother had stopped drinking alcohol completely though she drank a great deal of tea. A strong blend called Russian Caravan was her favorite. I seldom saw my father. Sometimes he would take me sailing, which seemed to make him more melancholy than ever. The sea was sullen and uncertain, some of the little coves he remembered so fondly were now reeking and silted. He still took some pleasure in his proficiency with the huge red sails, the ropes and pulleys, but the simple fragrance and freedom of his world had been lost to him, and so they were to me who had barely known them.

As for my mother, she was so convinced that I had died it was difficult for her to experience me as a living child. We spent long days in silence. Other times, days would pass with my mother speaking volubly about the diminishing fortunes of the world, the dystopian days ahead. Soon it will all be taken out of our hands, she said. What was it like there, she asked, the dead world? I tried to honor her queries for I loved her. She was my mother. It felt like the hour before daybreak, I told her, and she agreed that it would be like that. There were long figures above me, I told her another time. Were they like homes, she asked me, long homes? I think she must have read that somewhere, perhaps in one holy book or another. I tried to reassure my mother; I was polite and helpful, like a good guest. I probably should not have misled her.

"You're evolving," my mother said. "You don't want to just adapt, like me."

I did not feel as though I were evolving. My tutors found me simpleminded. The last one particularly found me exasperating.

"Do you have any idea why you're here?"

"I have to be here. Mother had a tutor and she . . ."

"No, here, on this earth." He raised his hands and cupped them as if he were holding something. He had the hands of an inept carpenter, the nails blackened and ridged.

"I don't have to answer that today," I said. "It doesn't have anything to do with spelling."

"Fine," he said. "If you just want to memorize definitions and crap that's fine with me, I'll still get paid. What is a homograph?"

"A word with the same spelling as another but with a different meaning." I liked homographs.

"How do you spell *commensurable?*"

Did he suspect I had forgotten how to spell it? I had not.

"How about *perspiration?*"

It was a word I liked very much.

"*Virus.*"

". . ."

"And what is a virus?"

"A virus isn't strictly alive but it isn't dead either. It's a life form."

"You are here on this earth to prepare a report on it," he said irritably. "What will be the nature of your report?"

"I don't know," I said.

"I've assisted other children," the tutor said. "I didn't come out of nowhere. But you must help me help you. Does the sun go around the earth or does the earth revolve around the sun?"

"The earth revolves around the sun."

"Why did people believe it was otherwise for so long?"

"Because it looks as though the sun is going around the earth."

"What is consciousness?"

"Consciousness is a dissociation of the I from the world of the not-I. It is a separation, a rift. No," I said. "That's not right."

"Your answer is adequate," he said impatiently.

"Why was the largest tree in our community cut down?"

He was being cruel bringing up the tree again. It always brought me close to tears. "Because it was in the middle of where they wanted to put the rotary," I said.

"No," he said. "It was because people suspected it felt it was going to live forever. What is God?"

"God is a way of thinking," I said meekly.

"We all lead three lives, the true one, the false one and what is the third?"

I said nothing.

"What is the third?"

"I don't know."

"I'm going to use the courtesy of the house," the tutor said, "and then I will return with your mother."

After a while the toilet flushed. Then he came back into the room with my mother. He was saying: "Most instructors wouldn't even take her on, you know. It's unlikely she'll ever be polished enough to address the real questions, the important ones. I am asking nothing of her but little baby steps." He looked at me. "Again, what is the third life?"

"Be imaginative, Khristen," my mother said. "Just guess."

"I don't want to guess."

"It's a riddle. Make something up."

"It's not a riddle."

"Well perhaps not. But listen. We all lead three lives. The true one, the false one, and the one we are not aware of. See how easy that was?"

At last the moment came when I was to be sent away to a real school, a boarding school in the West where my situation would be appreciated and the alarming gift I had been given properly acknowledged.

My mother told me that I was old enough to make the trip alone as there wasn't money for an additional fare.

In the beginning the only other passengers on the train were sociologists. They ignored me. There was nothing about me to inspire their interest. Still, their disappointment with one another was obvious. Each had hoped to encounter an artist, a poetic and drunken prelate, perhaps, a botanist, even a professional athlete or doomsday commentator. This is what the great trains of literature were supposed to provide. But all were sociologists, social workers, social engineers, sociobiologists.

"How did there get to be so many of us?" one of them said.

One of them commented on some peculiar ash-colored creatures in the distance, milling about in smoky disorder. "Look," he said, "beasts at play."

"Are they native to the region?" another asked. "They look rather rabid."

"I'm not sure what we're looking at," another one said.

If they hadn't all been sociologists, it might have occurred to them that the roily wonder were unprepared souls, moments from the clarity of their deaths, tumbling through terrifying illusions and deepening obscuration before their inescapable fall over the precipice into yet another suffering world.

But they were who they were. They couldn't think in an other-minded way. They turned from the window and regarded their dinner, which had been served. Collectively, they prodded the mass on their plates with their forks.

"What kind of fish is this supposed to be," one of them said. "It's not that damn orange roughy again I hope."

But it was, the waiter guessed, or had been.

Midway in the journey, additional parties boarded the train, including a girl my age and her mother. Picking up speed, the train tore past a truck parked under a dying cottonwood, a sign reading CAKES leaning against the tailgate.

"Isn't that fabulous," the mother said. "A bit of old Americana."

"You believe he's selling cakes," her handsome, pimpled child said. "He's not selling cakes, Mother."

"Oh stop," her mother said gaily. "Brittany's so suspicious of everyone," she announced. "You'd think somebody had smacked her with a board once. She wants to save the polar bears."

The girl's pimples reddened. "When did polar bears become funny, Mother? When did they become a punch line?"

"Oh stop. I don't know. I don't think they're funny. They're dangerous, aren't they? I remember it wasn't so long ago that you wanted to be a fashion designer."

"I have never never wanted to be a . . ." But her mother called out to a passing steward, "Come sit with us!"

"He works here, Mother," Brittany said. "He's an employee. He's not an enslaved companion like I am."

"Come join us!" the mother called out to me.

Brittany stared at me, dismayed. It was quickly confirmed that we would both be attending the same school.

"This was supposed to be a three-generational thing, this trip, but Mother died," Brittany's mother explained. "It was probably never that great an idea in the first place."

"Duh," Brittany said.

"It was her circulation, she'd had poor circulation for years."

"It's sad," Brittany said, "she had to die just to avoid going on this stupid trip."

"My grandmother died too," I said.

Brittany gazed at me and decided to allow no quarter.

"Generally that's what they do," she said. She turned to the window and wordlessly pointed out the Rio Grande.

Her mother said, "I heard it was much diminished."

"What have you left us?" Brittany demanded. "You haven't left us anything!"

"*I* didn't drain the Rio Grande, my dear."

"It's criminal," Brittany said.

"Tell me," her mother said, "when was the last time you read a good book by a polar bear?"

Brittany raised her hands in the air as though awaiting an assistant to prepare them for surgery.

"Would you like a glass of ginger ale or something?" the steward asked them.

"A glass of ginger ale would be just the thing," Brittany said, "unless you have a bottle of Tylenol PM and a quart of bourbon."

"Oh stop," her mother said, and laughed.

One of the social workers was heard expressing guilt about taking the time off. But they agreed they were all sick of their work—the smirking, nodded-out caregivers, the burns, the bruises, the shit in the snowsuits . . . They needed a break, this break.

"My clients are these kids who if you don't check on them weekly end up as discovered bodies in some storage box from Bed Bath and Beyond," another said. He then sneezed violently, twice, without apology.

Brittany rolled her eyes. She had a small notebook in which she wrote frequently. That morning, for instance, she had complained about the inconceivable absence of Weetabix at breakfast. It was a healthful given in this life, was it not, so why wasn't it available? In fact, why were so many staples becoming unavailable? I had a notebook, too, much like hers but nothing had been written in mine. I could tell that Brittany was thinking that if we became roommates she would positively die. She opened her notebook and with a silver pen wrote in it rapidly.

Her mother commenced speaking to me at length. Her name was Freida and she described herself as an eco-critic, an authority

on what she referred to as "the verge." The country was on the verge and had been for some time, the verge that people thought would go on forever. The hiking trails, the aquariums, the infertility treatments, the oxygen nutritional supplements continuing in cheerful tandem with the oil-soaked birds, the twelve-lane highways with bicycle supplements, the tailings dumps and filthy rivers and deserts blackened with solar panels, the billions of plastic bags translated in magical symbiosis into ethically responsible leisure equipment. Freida enjoyed a flourishing career addressing the verge, speaking at a variety of institutions to well-heeled, attentive and concerned yet complacent audiences. The *penurious rabble*—a term which Freida took pains to attribute to Hegel—were seldom in evidence, though they were a significantly significant component of the verge.

She took pride in her specialty and enjoyed explaining her work, which was to spiritualize the wants of consumers. Our spiritual development depended upon transcending nature. It is our moral destiny to technologically dominate the earth. The managed enhanced invented artificial environment would be quite lovely once the messiness was past.

It was rather a rip-off of Teilhard de Chardin, she admitted, but presented in a jollier, more digestible manner. In any case she made boatloads of money which was how she managed to send Brittany off for schooling.

"How did your family manage to afford the tuition?" she inquired.

"I think my mother put everything she perceived valuable on the block," I said.

"Ahh, things," Freida said dismissively. "What is your mother's profession?"

"She's a homemaker," I said uncertainly.

"Homemakers without homes," Freida said. "That is precisely our coming condition."

Terminating this lazy conversational exchange about my absent mother, she turned to Brittany.

"Can't you put something on those spots, dear?" she said, referring to the eruptions on her daughter's face.

"They're me, Mother," Brittany said.

"Oh they hardly *are*," Freida said.

The train sped over gulleys and draws through the warp and woof of blueing air changing to dark, a dull yellow light enveloping us all for an instant. The sociologists remarked passingly on the emptiness unaffected by the ten thousand human lives commencing every hour by most recent estimates.

Dinnertime had come and gone and we sat studying our desserts. Brittany pushed aside her dish holding a horridly browning pear half sunk in syrup and studied her notebook. These were her thoughts on a story called "The Overcoat" which had been assigned by a former preceptor. *We move overcoat by overcoat toward a dreadful end of which we never think . . . The author's characters are made half of flesh and blood and half of vapor, proof of the absurdity and futility that . . .* She crosshatched this out. A character in a story cannot be made of flesh and blood, not even half. She was astonished at how insincere she could be, but her mother was always questioning the authenticity of the authentic and urged her to do so as well.

Reflected in the window glass, everyone's plates were being removed.

"My daughter considers herself a post-humanist," Freida said.

Brittany stifled a gasp.

"I'm sorry, dear, but that is what you announced once." Then to our horror she winked at me.

This naturally destroyed any possibility of accord between Brittany and me. In our brief time together at school, Brittany mocked me to others as Sheep, as Mutton. She said I was a brain-dead dupe whose mind had quite possibly been spayed. I felt no

animosity toward her however. I could even admire the way she once argued in class that belief in the soul was nihilistic. It doesn't seem nihilistic, she said, but it is because then the ever more rapid destruction of the world doesn't seem so dreadful . . .

A star shot for a long time through the pale night. *"Grandma,"* Brittany said somberly. Another star fell down the night's dark throat. *"Grandma's little dog."*

. . . who had not long survived her death, the medicine upon which he relied—medicine which cost twenty dollars a day and which Champagne had already been on for over nine hundred days, with some serious side effects including extreme hair loss, gingivitis, and diarrhea—having been suspended. Her mother defended this decision by arguing that Champagne had long ago exceeded the median survival time for his progressive disease and was closing in on the upper range beyond which lay only the big cold kennel. She also pointed out that the only person who had unequivocally loved the difficult creature was gone, which would make a great difference in the quality of his life. So the medication was withdrawn and his decline was swift.

"Don't romanticize that Champagne," Freida said. "He didn't even want to be with Grandma as she lay there on her deathbed. He was always in the kitchen, whining under the table."

"There aren't meteors in meteor showers anymore," one of the sociologists proclaimed. "It's just space junk from rockets and satellites."

Brittany was searching for a fresh page in her notebook. There was the Overcoat again, which she made no attempt to conceal from me. *It is primarily a ghost story* . . . There were meticulous drawings of a sumptuous coat, wrapped around an idealized female form, the face hidden in the upraised collar.

She looked furtively at her mother and glared at me.

"The big question for your generation," her mother was saying, "is do you want to share the future or not?"

The train wicked something sizeable away from the tracks. An instant before, whatever it was had stood mesmerized by the single white eye of disturbing brightness hastening toward it.

The school was an old sanatorium surrounded by beetle-ravaged pines and staffed with nervous self-regard by arguably the cleverest minds in the country. Each student lived alone in a small spare room. All of them were children of divorce. It was practically a requirement. The place was monkish, the rooms always cold. There were no playing fields or gymnasiums. I realized I had somewhat been expecting gardens, laboratories and libraries. There were no books, no paper. One was simply supposed to remember the gnomic things the instructors uttered. Most schools told their captives many things without teaching them anything, filling them not with wisdom but the conceit of wisdom. This was wrong, I learned. Things would be different here.

At orientation in a cleared but stumpy patch of woods, a small professor with a resounding voice addressed us.

"What if a demon crept into your loneliest loneliness some day or night and said: 'This life as you live it at present and have lived it, you must live it once more and innumerable times after that and there will be nothing new in it but every pain and every joy and every sorrow and all the unspeakably small and great in your life must come to you again and all in the same series and sequence—and similarly this spider and this moonlight among the trees, and similarly this moment, and I myself.'"

A boy beside me began to cry; another muttered, "I don't want to be here. I had no say in the matter," while a third said, "Who asked to be born, not me." I had been so restricted in my dealings with others that I found this last complaint intriguing, much as I had marveled at the loudness of Freida's laughter.

The little man in the clearing continued.

"Would you not throw yourself down and gnash your teeth and curse this demon? Or would you experience a tremendous moment in which you would answer: 'You are a god and never have I heard anything so divine!' If the thought of this spider and this moonlight acquired power over you it would transform you and perhaps crush you for the answer to the question with regard to all and everything—do you want this all once more and also for innumerable times?—would lie as the heaviest burden upon your life. Or, cause it the greatest sanctified and eternally sealed joy."

"This is such a tremendous lot to ask of us," someone complained softly.

The student-inmates sat on benches in a sloppy circle. When there was complete silence once again, the professor, returning to the terror of his subject, screamed: "But I omitted a line!"

And the upperclassmen, all nine of them, screamed: "The eternal sandglass of existence will be turned again and thou with it, thou speck of dust!!!"

Nietzsche had always been the beginning and the end of the induction ceremony. It was a tradition.

The new students could not leave the campus for a year. We could not receive letters or packages, nor, naturally, could we send any. The instructors were distant, the texts obscure, the weather oppressive. The school was in a deep circular valley surrounded by dying trees. Many of the buildings and much of the furniture was crafted from the wood of these trees and had beautiful striated patterning, rivers of darkness almost purple in the pale grain. We knew nothing of the outside world's affairs, nor could we imagine what we were being groomed for. Perhaps the ruthless and painful requirements of nothing.

The place vanquished Brittany almost immediately. She burnt her beautiful notebooks and was taken away a shuddering ruin.

⚬✑⚬

Early in the winter of my second year, my mother, with great difficulty, broke through the communication prohibition with the news of my father's accident. Mothers die again and again, fathers but once, and my own father, on the threshold of that singular event, had been struck by a snapped winch in his boatyard.

"Him and those dreadful boats," my mother said.

I flew back across the country in an old plane that was being scrapped after this, her final flight. The passengers, upon hearing this announcement, applauded. The landing was exceedingly rough which the pilot blamed on people on the ground who were fooling around with lasers.

"Sometimes it's kids who don't realize the seriousness of what they're doing," he said. "Or it's gang members or people disposed to mischief and criminal behavior in general, or sometimes it's adults who've consumed hearty amounts of drugs or alcohol. Anyway, we made it. Have a nice day."

In the hospital room, my strong and capable father had been reduced to a crushed and twisted stranger. I was startled by the number of visitors there. One woman brought a small pillow with the words SPEEDS THE DAEDAL BOAT AS A DREAM in needlepoint and placed it beneath my father's cruelly swollen head. Too troubled to ask her what it meant, I went to the nurse's station and asked if they had a dictionary. "Not in this place, dear," one of them said.

"What is *daedal*?" I asked my mother.

"Ingeniously formed, skillful. From Daedalus who built the Cretan labyrinth. What are you learning at that school anyway?"

She ran her fingers through her hair and looked around the crowded room. "Who are all these people," she demanded. "Did he sleep with half the town?"

I didn't know them either though my mother seemed a stranger as well. Indeed, I almost wanted to sniff her, to smell her as an animal would her kind, for verification.

"Let's go to the cafeteria and have some cocoa," this creature said.

"I don't want any cocoa."

But we went down to the cafeteria in the bowels of the dreadful building, and sat at a Formica table upon which someone had etched in tiny script . . . HELL . . .

People at the other tables were staring into their computer screens. A teacher at school said that the online world—he called it *the online world*—employs only the parts of the brain that handle temporary fleeting minutiae and bulks up that part so that deep thinking is impossible, deeper understanding becomes elusive.

No one was weeping.

I stared at the letters. I put my hand over them, over *hell*.

"Your father never believed in you," my mother sighed. "Oh I'm not saying he didn't love you. He just didn't believe you'd been there, but I did. I knew you were special, a little chrisom child. And it used to weigh on me terribly. You were in some timeless future where you were charged with transformation and I had to keep you alive and it was hard, hard, you know, but now I have to ask you, what have you done with this information, what are you going to do with it?"

"I don't have any information, Mom." I realized that life never seemed more unreal than when I was with my mother.

"You don't think you're still there, do you, and this is all a misunderstanding? Because this is not a misunderstanding."

"Poor Daddy," I said.

"Oh yes," my mother said, blinking. "I'm beside myself, I guess that's obvious. Goodness. You're too skinny, why are you so skinny? Where are you staying? I'll give you money for a hotel. And there's some more, for school. But after that, no more. It's all gone."

"Can't I stay with you at home?"

"The house is gone, sold. It doesn't matter. I'm not going to stay in this town. I've said my good-byes to your father."

"How did you say them?"

My mother ignored this question. "I'm going to a visionary conference. It's at a resort on one of those enormous lakes your father loathed so much. But this one's much closer to where you are. It's only three hundred miles or so. We'll be neighbors practically!"

"I thought they were supposed to be pretty impractical," I said.

"Who?"

"Visionaries. That's the definition, isn't it?"

My mother looked at me. "It's quite a lineup and I'm giving it one last shot. It's not like anything I've tried before and I've tried everything as you might have guessed. There's going to be some new thinking at this conference. Pathways opening up to new solutions. There'll be scholars, scientists, lyricists, religious leaders there, the occasional party to keep our spirits up. I'm so fortunate to have heard about this. Try to be happy for me."

"No business leaders?"

"Of course not. Why are you being so unpleasant? These people are the new generation of guides. Very qualified. I'm going to audit all the panels, as many as I can. I don't care about the credits. I don't need the credits."

"I thought my school was supposed to be full of guides."

"Oh I don't know about that now. I guess not. That place isn't as eminent as it used to be. I got a little behind on my research. I wish I had hypnotists work with you when you were a toddler, Lamb. You're continuing to be denied access to the most important part of your life, the future you had in death! I think you're just being stubborn."

She was called away then for a moment and when she returned, she said, "He's gone."

I was afraid I would not see my mother again, or it might be more accurate to say I was afraid that were we to meet, I would not recognize her, which is far more terrible, a terrible thing. But she said she would come to the hotel the following day and we would go to a small memorial service for my father and then the gravesite, for the dead are buried quickly now.

I do not know how I managed to pass the night. When I descended to the lobby the following afternoon I noticed a television screen over the reception desk. A film was running of a large bird making careful refinements to a coarsely built nest. I watched it for a time uneasily.

"Weren't you watching that yesterday?" the clerk asked.

"No."

"But you noticed the pole outside when you checked in, didn't you? Big pole with a platform on top, camera on another pole angled toward it? Hard to miss."

"This is real time, then?"

"Well it was," the clerk said. "But she flew into a truck or something. Or the mate couldn't find fish. Weather's been crappy, unsettled, water's cloudy. There are any number of theories."

"So when was this?"

"A year ago at least."

"But why are you still showing it?"

"Isn't that self-evident?" he said. "Most people like looking at it."

I turned my back on the film and on the fastidious and useless preparations being recorded there and sat on a divan before a table on which lay an untidy stack of newspapers. The divan was uncomfortable but I must have dozed because I felt startled awake when a woman sat down heavily beside me.

"Do you know what day it is?" she asked.

"I do. Very much."

"My Marie would have been fifteen years of age today." She tapped the newspaper on top of the pile with a gnawed, not very clean finger. It was open to the obituary page and the finger was being directed to a black-bordered memoriam of a child in a sun-suit holding a book upside down. Having noted first the book, the title of which was not legible, and the blonde ringleted child only later, I felt at an immediate disadvantage.

"Two," the woman said. "I've been doing this for thirteen years now and I'll be doing it thirteen more if I'm still drawing breath. It's working out pretty well. Lots of people know her now, hundreds. She's not so shy anymore. She used to be wicked shy. She didn't like to have her picture took."

"I'm sorry," I said.

"Imagine her a little. Like what would she be doing right now?"

I shook my head.

"Wouldn't cost you nothing to imagine this child," she said. "I'm not asking for the skin off your back!" She was rocking back and forth and seemed to be revolving at the same time. "It would be a big help to Marie," she cried. "She appreciates it. Marie wouldn't be nothing without your help."

I said, "She's drinking apple juice. It tastes good. She's enjoying a moment by herself."

The woman scowled. "Why would she want to be by herself?"

"She's in a pretty seaside garden, she's planting bulbs," I said without hope.

"Too late in the year for bulbs," she said.

"Marie," I said.

"Yes," she said, not brightening in the slightest. "I'm glad she didn't live to see all this fakery. Everyone pretending things will be all right. You pretending." Primly, she folded up the paper and went to the lobby's desk where she conferred with the clerk. He

appeared to be sympathetic to what she was saying. Perhaps she was a palace pet. Many public spaces have them, I'd been told. Perhaps she brought luck to those who helped her in small ways. They both looked at me with disappointment. Above them in its aerie the bird was turning a brown, prettily mottled egg with her beak.

I went outside to wait for my mother. I sat at a table and was presented with a glass of water. I moved to pick it up but it fell from my hand toward the floor. I watched it falling in a sort of trance. In that moment of its falling I knew my mother would never arrive.

Eventually I found my way to the boatyard where the mourners had gathered. They were not the same people I had seen in the hospital. The food and drink had been consumed and they were now in the process of carrying everything out of my father's lodging. They did not address me or even look at me. They pocketed the silver, rolled up the rugs and removed the glasses and blankets. My father had few books. I recalled him reading little other than those on boats and boat-building. He had enjoyed all commentary on the sea, taking particular note of captains who had been relieved of their command or who, in disgrace, had been reassigned. These volumes, too, were taken.

Though these were terrible omens, I felt my only recourse was to return to studies I could not comprehend and trust that the future would eventually disclose itself as it had to all beings in the past.

Back at school I tried to describe the mourners' behavior to a classmate.

"That couldn't have happened that way," Jack said. "People coming into your dead dad's place and taking everything."

"Everything."

"All at once and without saying a word? . . . They take up a collection for you?"

"They did not."

"I've heard of wakes getting out of hand but nothing like this. That's some seriously disordered mourning."

"I don't think this was a wake."

"You want me to help figure this out or not? It was a festivity. People were eating and drinking and walking around talking about the deceased. That's a wake. But then they up and robbed you of all the stuff you were supposed to inherit. It's just the damnedest thing."

Jack was a caring boy, not lachrymose and knowing like his two sisters who had time-shares in Ohio and North Carolina respectively—that is, they were still in prison. He had brought his powder-coated El Camino to school along with all the parts he'd been accumulating, the second engine, the vent window gaskets, the tail-light housings, the two doors complete with glass. But he was not allowed to work on it and was forbidden to drive it.

"You know the lion cub that was supposed to be coming to the zoo back where I'm from?" he said. "The one from the other zoo? The one I've been telling you about and waiting on to see when I get out of here? It's not coming now since the zoos have been washed away."

He confessed that he was at a loss as to what he could look forward to now.

He clandestinely installed photo paper on a wall in his room with a black-maned lion looking for all the world like it was striding down a darkened hallway right toward you.

The same questions were being asked but more unrelentingly.

*Why are you here? Why are you here? What is the purpose of human life on this earth?*

The classroom was cold. One of the instructors was speaking and his breath was visible in the air. I studied the reindeers romp-

ing over my mittens. Many of my clothes had once belonged to a much younger child.

There was a pause and a student said, "I was peeling an orange this morning and I noticed that the peel I was about to throw into the garbage reminded me of squamous cells, those tiny epidermal flakes that fall off our skin. I then realized that without knowing it we all of us are sowers who spread tiny particles of skin here and there along our path. We create with our very waste."

"Interesting," the instructor said.

"Where'd you get an orange?" another student demanded. "I haven't tasted an orange in years."

"Yeah, where'd you get an orange!" several challenged.

"It's an *example*," the boy said. "I'm offering an example." He muttered, "I wasn't really peeling an orange."

"Interesting," the instructor said again, "but we are not discussing creativity. We are discussing the state. Let us return to the state. We are dominated by large organizations, governments, churches, industrial and financial giants. All these are large and they grow larger as the dinosaurs did. It is visible to everyone that their level of intelligence and their ability to look into the future are exceedingly small. They cannot change, they can only expand. As long as there was room and the means to expand they could thrive. But now it is no longer possible to expand. Growth in this way is impossible. Now it is not merely a duty but a necessity to control, to restrain and to concentrate."

"Is individual growth possible?" someone questioned.

"No."

With this, the class was dismissed.

"He is so boring," the boy beside me whispered, "but he's so cute."

In the dining hall, supper was powdered eggs and toast again. It was the fifth evening this had been so. The school had been in

some disarray ever since the disappearance of a senior scholar, the Caliph the students called him. He was an avid hiker and climber and the fear was that he had fallen or encountered some mishap in the mountains. Some of the teachers set out to search for him— they wouldn't allow the students to accompany them—but they found no trace of him.

"Well I always found him somewhat repellent," a girl named Lucinda said. "His person as well as his mind. Someone probably murdered him because he was so repellent."

"I never understood a thing he said," Jack offered.

"He would have been disappointed if you had," Lucinda said. "If any of us had."

"I've been thinking," Jack said to me, "what happened at your dad's place? That wasn't a wake, it was a burglary."

"I adore that word," Lucinda said. "*Burglarious* is even better. Like *This burglarious place is sucking out our souls.*" She had briefly been Brittany's roommate and had outmaneuvered her at every turn.

"Do you know what *daedal* means," I asked.

"Sure," Lucinda said.

No one believed the scholar had been murdered. Lucinda was just being playful. He had suffered a tragic fall was the gradually accepted opinion, somewhere in the unforgiving mountains.

It was becoming apparent that in the Caliph's absence, the school was unraveling. People spoke of him in the present tense to no avail. I was in my third year now, a junior, but the class above me did not have the opportunity to scream at the freshmen: *The eternal sandglass of existence will be turned again and thou with it, thou speck of dust!!* There was no incoming class. Everyone missed the tradition of this spider and this moonlight though the distinction between reincarnation and recurrence remained blurry for some. I

felt that if I had to relive once more my time here since my father's death and my mother's disappearance, it would be as perplexing as before—the horrid food, the mysterious lectures, the childish outfits everyone wore, the enshrinement of doubt. I would not feel joyfully sanctioned. I had learned nothing and could not recognize an illusion from my left hand.

The situation in the world outside our sheltered if dreary valley had changed, we were told. Priorities had changed. Hence the lack of an incoming class. But there were even more pressing problems. There was talk of a third of the once familiar world outside us being gone. A third of the whole. The remainder was still manageable, it was rumored; in fact things had to be managed more than ever. The two thirds left couldn't be a whole, strangely enough.

More and more classes were canceled. We would meet at dusk in one of the school's many courtyards discussing the sounds that had been going on for weeks.

It sounded like cars, trucks backfiring.

A number of cars or trucks backfiring for a considerably long time.

That's what people say gunfire sounds like.

Nobody says that anymore.

It didn't sound like guns at all, more like explosions.

Prolonged explosions.

What about the smell?

The odor?

It was more like thunder, rolling, rolling thunder.

Mother Nature batting last.

Nobody says that anymore.

Then it was announced that the campus would be closed for a newly determined holiday. The explanation was that they were going to paint the dormitories, replace the boiler, modernize the kitchen and build a library. No one even bothered to refute these

ridiculous claims. The last meal was a breakfast of powdered eggs and toast. Grim-faced parents arrived for their children in monster trucks hauling elaborate travel homes or in waxed limousines. Jack's sisters (who had been released from prison) arrived, and they all left in the El Camino, though the additional parts had to be left behind. All the prisons had been emptied, the opera houses and theaters closed. Lucinda's parents picked her up in a hearse. They were funeral "directors" and had more money and business than God, Lucinda always said. She invited me to go with her but I demurred.

"I like you," Lucinda said. "You have no self-love. But you don't have any sense of self-preservation either, which I hate to admit is very important to me. I don't think we'll see each other again."

We'd heard that the only businesses operating on the outside were casinos where Indians who'd lost their great-grandfathers to smallpox, whose great-grandmothers' bones resided in the basements of collapsed museums, now enforced the rules, such as they were.

I was the only one escorted to the train station. There was a large painting of a harrow on the wall. "That's new," my instructor commented. "Sure looks official, doesn't it." The waiting room was deserted. "A parent will be meeting you at the other end, is that right?" the instructor said.

"Yes," I said.

"The parent knows you're coming?" He'd heard that one of them had died but damned if he could remember which one. His short-term memory was increasingly failing him. He blushed. He knew he was considered the boring one, the cute one, which was bad enough, but now he had to face the realization that he was getting dumber and more irrelevant with each passing day. He felt faintly euphoric. He was surprised that the trains were still running.

cℐℴ

The train lacked a dining car, nor were there sleeping compartments. The lavatories were locked. A dozen people rocked sullenly in broken seats. No one spoke. They slept with their eyes open as the first night passed void of stars. The land was bright with raging fires ringed by sportsmen shooting the crazed creatures trying to escape the flames. The train pushed forward, if fitfully, on designated tracks. It sped by stations but stopped beside empty fields enclosed in wire. Passengers would disembark and not reboard. It stopped where the man and his sign marked CAKES still waited. He darted into the car with a large tray of sweets that were colorfully decorated but hard as stone. People bought them and jammed them into their mouths anyway.

For a time, the train kept sluggish pace with a livestock truck and its cargo of shifting dappled bodies.

The moment I realized that I alone remained on board, the train stopped for good. I climbed down and walked through brittle grasses and over cracked earth until the tracks were no longer visible. I came upon a little grove that was surprisingly green and freshly pleasant except for the packages of meat dumped there. They were wrapped tightly in slim plastic, the cut's name and weight and the price stamped on a strip of paper that was separated from the meat by an absorbent pad now pink.

A man pulling a cross appeared on the crest of a hill and started down it toward the grove. The butt of the cross rested on a duffel bag tied to a board that was mounted on two wheels. He approached, unsmiling. The cross was sixteen feet long and made from what looked like Styrofoam painted black.

"Good morning," he said, although it was almost night. "Alleluia." He laid the cross down carefully. "People who know me call me the Convertor but I tell strangers to call me Larry so they'll feel more comfortable." He explained that he was coming up from

the south where people still believed, but in the most perfunctory manner. For years he had been traveling back and forth across the country and he would continue to do so, doing God's work until he was informed that it was done. In these days of woe, more and more people were informing him that it was done.

"I even got beat up as you can see," Larry said. "Got some of my teeth knocked out."

He opened his mouth wide and a terrible odor issued forth which dissipated leisurely. He closed his mouth and spoke through barely parted lips again.

"Where you headed?"

"I'm not sure," I said.

"Yup, that's the answer I get most frequently. You are not alone. That is, you're alone of course but there's others in a likewise situation is what I mean."

We regarded the meat. There seemed even more of it than there had been before.

"Troubling," Larry said, "in this pleasant place of respite. Seems I just saw that beef when they was cows."

We looked at the meats bulging and browning against the constraints of their packaging.

"Ezekiel!" Larry cried in a weak and wavering voice, "Ezekiel was set down in the valley of dry bones by the Lord who said to him 'Can these bones live?' and Ezekiel figured well probably no. But then the Lord *laid sinews upon them and flesh and breathed into them and they did live . . .*" He raised his hands and waggled them. "Amen," he said. "But those were bones," he added. "There was something to work with."

Then, with more effort than habit and appearance might suggest, he lifted the cross to his shoulder and labored off.

❧

My mother had said, "Even if I was mistaken that night and you didn't cross over the shadow line, the borderland, do you ever feel that you have died and are walking among those who might have died as well but are not telling?

"Because," my mother said, "no one tells."

I thought about that now, as the days I moved through seemed hesitant, as though waiting for something further and not to their benefit to be decided. The people I saw didn't seem to be traveling. They were milling, like little flies after a rain. Hope no longer found a place to dwell. Even the insects felt it gone. The colt, the cub, the calf, the stones that would be precious jewels deep within the earth. The flowers who, as Wordsworth knew, enjoyed the air they breathed, were aware of nothing but hope's absence. Something definitely had gone wrong. Even the dead were dismayed.

But then the dead commenced to regain their bearings, their sea legs as it were, and those close to death and the unborn as always. As for the others, they hardly cared who or what it was that was pleading with them now, for everything seemed less touching than before.

For a time I was on a wide highway that had been in the process of being widened further, though a series of stanchions had narrowed it to a single track. No vehicles passed. A gas station attendant told me that only commerce slash security slash essential slash emergency services got fuel, and that temporarily—only on Thursdays and every other Tuesday.

"People are calm though," he said. "If you're not calm there's immediate custody which is not pretty, I've seen it. It's a matter of attitude. If you've got the right attitude you're going to be fine."

Someone on the road offered me a look through his binoculars which he carried in a pouch around his neck. They were well cared for. Beneath the protective caps the glass was unscratched.

A white capsule in the pouch said THROW AWAY DO NOT EAT. But it had not been thrown away.

"Keeps the fungus from getting on the glass," the man said.

The land looked torn, turned inside out.

At times, moving forward, I pretended I was heading home, like a bird or animal might, stubbornly, to a place it had known for many seasons, the previous season being an exception, the extinction of the place, an exception. Birds and animals must feel like this, I imagined, harboring a faith that only the saints must know, a faith that cannot be betrayed but only transformed. But when I could no longer think of myself, much as I longed to, as a bird or an animal, I grew weary and uncertain. I was not returning home.

A group of adolescents overtook me. They were pushing or riding bicycles and resembled my former classmates not at all.

"Jesus, these little flies," one girl protested, rearranging a dirty scarf around her face.

"There are flowers that want to be pollinated by flies," a boy said. "They stink so bad only the flies will come to them."

"Flies don't pollinate flowers," the girl said.

"Yes, they do."

"Creep," the girl said.

"You going to the party house?" one of them asked me.

"Is it on a large lake?" I asked.

"No lakes around here," a boy said. "Maybe further on."

"Yes, there's a humongous one further on," a girl said. "But I don't think it's there anymore."

"She doesn't know anything about it obviously," the boy assured me. "Are you a student?"

"I was."

"We're students at large," he said. "The world is our classroom." They all laughed harshly at this.

"We've had lots of learning experiences," one offered.

"Like we were camping and this guy we didn't know was

there—he was there ahead of us actually—and he was staring at this rock. He stared at it so long that the rock felt threatened I think and it rose up and struck him and killed him."

"I like the rocks we find with the holes in them," a boy said.

"Who doesn't, moron, but here's our situation. We're learners and seekers but we don't know what we're searching for. We don't have the words, or the words we have are the wrong ones. And it can't be otherwise."

"True!"

"The ones who came before us, they named the animals, the flowers, the trees, the lowliest bush. But they weren't the right ones. So now it doesn't matter when all that's gone."

"That's our purgative."

"Prerogative, asswipe. What's important is we're men. Both as individual and horde we are . . ."

"Men!"

"That's right. Even the ladies. Capable of anything!"

They called themselves the Fallout and they invited me to accompany them to a place they called the party house, a place they had been frequenting and were tenderly nostalgic about. This was how they described their feelings about the place to me— *tenderly nostalgic.*

"It's like your granddaddy's house," they explained to me, "if you'd had one of those dear make-believe granddaddys."

The party house was a farmstead where an old professor had been dying for some time. Whenever they arrived he thought they'd come to take care of his beloved horses, but there weren't any horses. If ever there had been they must have starved or wandered out of the collapsed barns and through the open fencing long ago.

Some of the girls in the group believed the professor realized there were no horses but knew that admitting this would be the end of him. The boys didn't understand why he wouldn't want

his end to come. He wasn't stupid. He was crippled and old—God, he was older than anyone they'd ever met—and if he persisted, someone could come by and take advantage of him, hurt him, maybe even murder him, and he would die disillusioned.

"Yeah, but everyone dies disillusioned," one of the girls said. She carried a desert tortoise in an open picnic basket. A green swastika was painted on its shell, not the Nazi swastika but its reverse, one of the most ancient and complex symbols of history.

"Some people look at this and freak," the girl said. "They think we're marauding skinheads."

"That's just a shell," I said.

"Yeah, it's a desert tortoise."

"She's not in there anymore," I said. "She's been removed."

Another girl said, "Some researcher in California wanted us to send her there so she could hook up with this tortoise boy they got. You know how they get a tortoise to shoot his little tortoise wad when he's not so inclined? They give him an electric shot."

Shock, she was corrected.

"But we said no, no," she went on, "we won't give her up because you might not send her back, that's what we said to the researcher in California."

"We used to think she was lucky but now we don't," a boy said, regarding the domed shell, "since somebody who will remain nameless and is no longer with us scooped her from her home to see what she looked like and then of course she didn't look anything like what she really was . . ."

"But we're not going to abandon her," the girl carrying the basket said. "We're sweethearts. That's why we play along with the professor. 'Your students have come back to take care of your horses,' we tell him. 'We're the farriers returning from the age of iron,' we say."

"He might be dead this time around though. You can't live on pain pills forever at that age."

"But we can," a boy said. "We metabolize them better."

The Fallout were cheerful, ruthless, resourceful, self-absorbed and undespairing. Despair, they explained to me, was caused by the attempt to live a life of virtue, justice and understanding. Despair arose when one tried to understand and justify human existence and behavior. This was the most important thing they had learned as students. It used to be you had to be a small child, practically an infant, or awakened and enlightened in the extreme to be legitimately undespairing, but they scoffed at such restrictions. The Fallout certainly weren't babies, nor would they be the resigned and ingravescent old. They doubted they'd last the year out. They didn't care.

"Where did you get the bicycles?" I asked.

A boy admitted they'd belonged to unfortunate children who had drowned for lack of a ladder. The tanks were everywhere to catch and hold water—you must have noticed them, he said—but only the old ones had ladders. The tanks had once been rather beautiful but in time they'd collapsed and the new ones were uglier, larger and progressively more crude. Building an escape ladder had always been one of the cardinal rules of construction, though the guardians of these children, in their haste, had frequently forgotten this.

Some of the bikes bore colorful decals of wizards and skulls, tornadoes, panthers straddling rockets. "A lot of these kiddies were military issue," a boy explained, "copying their daddies' secret program patches."

"Secret, Secret, Secret," the Fallout yipped.

And so I accompanied them yipping and laughing to the party house, an arid farm surrounded by dead orchards. The professor was still in living residence and the Fallout found this delightful. They greeted him and exclaimed over the continuing good health of his horses, after which they retired into the back reaches of his property for their self-medicating regimens.

The professor was sitting in a checkered wing chair with what looked like a tablecloth over his knees. The window was open and a wind pushed moodily around in the dusk.

" 'He's mad that trusts in a horse's health,' " he said. "*King Lear*. Are you one of my students?"

"No," I said.

"The ones who were just here tell me they are, but I can see right through them as the saying goes."

"I would like to learn but I can't seem to."

"Have to know the proper channels, though the channels are always shifting and don't stay proper for long. But I'm pretty much out of commission as a pilot. I took quite a tumble and at my age when the bones break they stay broken. Where did you come from? Where were you born?"

I named the town on the coast and the word seemed awkward in my mouth. Oddly, in that moment, I had a memory of mispronouncing the word *detritus*. It's *de try tus* for heaven's sakes, one of my teachers had scolded.

"You're not trying to return there, are you?" asked the professor. "You'll find it much changed."

"No, I'm not going there."

"I believe they're strictly limiting entry though exceptions can always be made. The courts are all there now."

"I don't have a destination really."

"Probably because there aren't any. To have one was always rather a luxury."

"The last time I saw my mother she said she was going to a facility on a large lake where a visionary conference was taking place. Perhaps you heard of it?"

He smiled. "So many conferences and congresses. They were so in vogue a while back. Certainly the past is merely a grammatical construct, but that really was some time ago."

"My mother says that time observes me differently because I was dead for a while."

"Yes, well that will do it," the professor said blandly. "I was honored at an environmental conference there, their last one. Loss was the theme. Reflections on loss. Ways to navigate loss. The opportunities in loss. How to make loss work for you . . . What a bunch of fruitcakes. There was one panel . . . I don't have the program after all this time, but I remember the title very clearly, the title is just dancing in the air before my eyes, I can see it more clearly than I see you, even." He made as if to scribble in the air with his finger. *"The Potentiality of Landscape's Emptiness: The Integrity of Half Measures."*

"What were they honoring you for?"

"My area of expertise, all the little grasses. I spent my life studying grasses. I liked the prairie grasses best. They once could have survived the worst, you know, whether fire or ice, their roots went so deep. That's what the worst was thought to be once—freeze and flame. They were eradicated instead by simple human commitment, that and the fact that the determination to survive that other forms of life ofttime exhibit impels many people to extremes of destruction." He fussed with the cloth on his lap. "Regardless," he said, "I couldn't attend the conference, the obsequies. I'd taken my final spill, my last fall. It was like missing my own funeral." He glanced at the window and quickly away. "You're a patient little thing, aren't you, to have no idea how long ago that was."

There was the sound of distant laughter and the faint smell of smoke.

"They're going to burn whatever's left down one of these nights," he said. "Do me a favor, would you, shut that window over there. That was the horses' favorite window. They'd stick their big heads in and visit with me. But they don't anymore. If

you're blessed enough to save something, it doesn't stay saved, are you aware of that?"

The window wouldn't budge. I tried to rock it in its frame. The glass was old, thick, voluted.

"Watch out for splinters," the professor warned. "When I was a little boy my best friend died of defenestration. He was fascinated with windows. He thought there was another world out there and people were forever trying to convince him it was the same one. He was an exceptionally frustrated child. The possibilities of the window were for him the only possibilities that mattered. Death by jumping out a window was a cause of death just made for Woodrow. Well he found his window in the tallest building in town. It was only four stories high but he was dashed to pieces of course. His mother permitted the harvest of some of his bones for cadaver wafers. Someone talked her into it. Now there's no telling how many people with osteoarthritis of the spine—desperate enough to assent to the surgeon's knife—have a bit of Woodrow's cartilage in them. Knowing that would disappoint him, I'm certain. He didn't care for people much. Not that he was a mean boy, he just wasn't charitable, and his bones ended up wafting around in others, helping others. Goodness, I haven't talked this much in years."

The window came down abruptly, meeting the rough sill.

"I thought it would make more of a fuss," he said.

The room seemed thunderously still with the window shut.

"Quiet, isn't it," the professor noted. "As if we've been punched right back to the Middle Ages, a time characterized by a quality of silence quite unimaginable today. That's why music then had an almost supernatural power." He sighed. "Thank you, dear, I've indulged myself quite long enough. I should have gone where you're going when I had the chance but our lives don't move in a horizontal fashion anymore, perhaps they never did. I took my disability far too seriously and the years proceeded, the

calamities piled up. I'm truly incapacitated now, wouldn't be able to serve. Lola won't let anyone die there, that's one of her rules. She runs a tighter ship."

"Who's Lola?"

"Why she's in the place you seek, the facility, as you so formally and politely called it, on the lake. Your mother's last resort is under new management now. No more of this rational-use, academic-integrated approach, sustainable-compromise crapola. Lola steers a different vessel under a different star."

"But I'm not looking for her," I said. The room was suffocating with the window closed but had a faint familiar smell, like crushed leaves.

"Woe when you feel homesick for the land and there is no longer any land," he said. "But that's where you're headed, I'm fairly certain, and Lola will have to do. Now I want you to take my truck. I have a fine old truck in that blue outbuilding you passed. I used it for years to trailer my babies here. It's in the cellarage. Just open the doors down there. I'd love to think that Lola will welcome you but it's quite possible she won't. But such a loss at this point hardly matters, does it."

"I don't know," I said.

BOOK TWO

Come, I can use you, said the peculiar stranger.

—"KIENAST"
ROBERT WALSER

This is the way the world looks.
The world looks . . . trashed.

—WILLIAM GASS

Poor old Big Girl. A crow could not be made blacker than her sick waters. The setting sun regarded her and threw a half-hearted shimmer over her flabby surface. For an instant she turned a promising silver. When someone is dying, humming rolling and cracking noises wheel around the body for up to fifteen hours, unheard and unacknowledged. It is a scientific fact, though suppressed. Big Girl had popped and droned and shrieked and snapped for years as was often the case with water, but had been silent now for just as long.

A woman holding a martini glass stood beside a child on the shore. The boy had caught a small fish and was looking at it unhappily.

*You can't start thinking that fish has a story, Jeffrey,* the woman said, her hand on the rod's line from which the fish feebly struggled. *That way lies madness.*

The fish was not rose-moled stippled and lovely but gray and gaunt as though it had lived its brief life in a drainpipe.

*This fish is part of your story only, Jeffrey,* the woman continued. *This lake is here to produce fish for your pleasure and repulsion and to instill in you a sense of power and pity.*

She turned, the martini glass deftly turning with her, and looked behind her.

*What are you staring at!* she snapped.

WHAT'S YOUR NAME AGAIN?" LOLA ASKED. "YOU'RE NOT OLD enough to be part of the Institute. You don't even look as though it's your destiny to join in a great experience."

"Oh!" Khristen laughed, embarrassed.

"It's one of my favorite first lines in literature. *It was my destiny to join in a great experience.* Of course the narrator was utterly mistaken. Human destiny has quite played itself out. You don't have to agree of course. But it's so lovely you brought Julian's truck! Maybe we'll start the tours again—they were very popular. Some prankster drove our previous vehicle into the lake and the silt swallowed it."

"Who gave the tours?" Khristen asked.

"Oh, one of us," Lola said vaguely. "Most of our arrivals come via Mr. Stroup. I know Honey did. Mr. Stroup used to be a preacher. He preached a lot on the seven bowls when that was in vogue. Then he was an electrician, one of those unlicensed ones you use in desperation. He had a white van. It used to be an ambulance but the only thing that remained in it from its heyday was the tip jar. But Stroup hasn't been by for a while."

"What are the seven bowls?"

"The seven horrifying judgments, the ones that show no restraint. The seven gleaming bowls full of the wrath of God. Plague, war, the destruction of great cities, heat, the dying of the oceans, endless darkness."

"But that's only six," Khristen said.

Lola laughed loudly. She was tall, with blurred features except for her prominent eyes. "You're a quick one, I can never do all seven. One always escapes me."

"That's all right," Khristen said.

They were sitting on what Lola referred to as the "veranda" on the destitute grounds of the razed resort. The lake, which had taken on mythic proportions in Khristen's mind, was not visible, but a small neatly maintained motel was. Behind the veranda a half-demolished building leaned toward them as though listening.

"Tell me about the professor. Poor Julian's a sad tale. Were any of the horses still there?"

"The people who were visiting him were pretending there were horses but I didn't see any."

"Oh he had so many of them! Percherons they were. Premarin foals. There was a hormone that pharmaceutical interests got from the urine of pregnant mares that was much in demand but there was no use for the resultant foals, which were just shipped off to slaughter. It was a big business and probably will be again. There's no expiration date on the resourcefulness of greed and cruelty. Julian rescued, oh, at least a hundred of them to my knowledge, though he never caught up to the reality of the numbers. He was an expert on grasses, really had a way with them. Of course the foals could obliterate a meadow with their sinless crushing jaws in no time and the irony of the situation depressed him terribly. No horses at all? He loved them so. They used to stick their big heads in the window of his bedroom. I believe they loved him too. Wish we could have gotten him over here when he was still mobile. He's just going to die for nothing now."

In the distance, past neglected gardens, was an enormous crumbling amphitheater. Lola pointed toward it.

"That environmental conference you spoke of, dear, the one you said your mother was pilgriming off to, that was a very long

time ago you have to realize. Time doesn't have the tolerance with us that it used to. For all the good it did, that conference could have taken place before you were born."

Lola was in agreement with the old professor's memory of the place. A large meeting of the usual maundering and hypocritical leaders had occurred before the total abandonment of civilized, if fruitless, discussion. Khristen was no doubt an orphan by now, sharing that designation with a primary part of the populace and most of the non-human inhabitants of what was still classified, mostly out of laziness, as the natural world.

"Are you hungry?" Lola asked.

"I am very hungry," Khristen admitted.

Lola looked disappointed.

"We have dinner at seven but few attend. They've all got ailments of course and special diets are impossible. Some of them can't even eat a mashed potato."

"I could."

"If you could hang on until tomorrow the little boy staying at the motel with his mother is having a birthday party and there should be cake at least."

"I believe I saw them," Khristen said. "He had caught a fish."

"A fish!" exclaimed Lola. "Was it rotting from the tail up?"

"I wasn't that close to see. It didn't look rotting. It was mostly head though."

"That's quite remarkable," Lola said, "that he would catch a fish. To dream of a fish means death, you know. What did he do with it?"

"He wanted to put it back but I'm not sure if he did, they didn't want to be observed, I think."

"That woman has quite the dilemma. Actually if you attended little Jeffrey's birthday party it would be much appreciated. I know Barbara is less than pleasant but she's got a lot on her mind. The boy's father murdered his grandfather recently and since the child

is not aware of this, she feels she's raising him under a cloud. She wants him to be a lawyer. Both his father and grandfather were lawyers and you may well ask what good it availed them but she's insistent. She's trying to keep him focused on the future. Torts, she told me, is his destiny."

"Torts," Khristen repeated. She thought it meant twists. To some degree turns. Twists and turns foreseen as design. It was nice that the child's mother was admitting for him such freedom; she hadn't seemed to be the type.

"You just hang on until tomorrow. You're welcome to stay for a night or two though you're not at all qualified. Frankly those of your age are anathema to our whole concept. We don't want to be responsible for you. We do pity you, however. Anyway, I'll find something for you here. We all stay in that building. The motel's just for show."

"That building doesn't look safe," Khristen ventured.

"Safe! Well, we don't go out on the balconies much."

Indeed the balconies did not look as if they would suffer to be enjoyed.

"I'll make you head of housekeeping, perhaps," Lola said. "This would not involve any mundane cleaning of rooms of course. You seem a lovely girl. Most people carry their ultimate end around with them like a stepchild they're reluctant to acknowledge, but you don't."

"My mother said . . ."

Lola raised one pale hand dismissively. "I harbor no prejudice against the woman but she obviously wasn't the one for you."

"We only get one mother."

"All the more reason, even if it were true. Do you think there's a certain time for everything and a certain season and all will be well and all will be well and all will be well?"

"Not really."

"Let me tell you a little story. When this place was going good,

wildlife biologists would rent blocks of rooms for weeks at a time and do research on the herons and egrets which were plentiful then. They'd go out to the bird colonies on the little islands in airboats, knock as many birds as they could off their nests with tranquilizing darts, fit them with solar-powered radio transmitters attached to little backpack harnesses and release them. Then they'd track them by airplane and learn what they could learn. One evening they came back with this little tricolored heron that they thought they had fatally overdosed, not their intention of course. They kept it in a box and poked and prodded it through the night hoping for a sign of life and there was none. But some time just before daybreak, one of the researchers heard a weak scratching emanating from the box and when she turned on the light, much to her amazement, there was the heron looking at her. They called the heron 144 which was the frequency of the radio signal they fitted her with and released her in the vicinity of her nest which, unattended, had unsurprisingly collapsed. They lost contact with 144 almost immediately. She vanished from the search area. They never found her."

After a moment, Khristen said, "It doesn't sound as if it were ever nice around here."

"Those biologists paid in cash and always messed up the plumbing," Lola mused. "And they were so smug about those damn harnesses. They claimed they were designed to allow complete freedom of flight as well as all other activities."

"I don't believe that, do you?" Khristen said.

Dirty-looking clouds passed over them in a lofty rack. "They do that every afternoon around this time," Lola said. "Go to squat above the lake."

"That is such a sad story," Khristen said.

Lola looked surprised. "That little tricolored heron thwarted those people. I always found it quite inspiring."

A truck hauling a bass boat roared noisily up to them, filming

Khristen's bare legs with dust. The driver, with little ceremony, inquired as to how the hell he could access the frigging lake, he'd been driving for hours and seen no break in the fucking dike.

"You can access it from here," Lola said, "but you've got to pay for a room. I don't care if you use it or not, spend the night or not, but you've got to pay for it."

"I'm not paying for shit!" the man hollered. He cursed the establishment and sped away.

"I'm going to rest," Lola said wearily. "I'm tuckered. I've got the cancer down to my fingertips, down to my very bunions—no need to commiserate. Whyn't you take Room Five, that's on the other side of the breezeway from Honey, Heart of Gold. You'll meet her. Nothing to be afraid of there."

"It's too late to be afraid, I think," Khristen said.

"Why that's so true," Lola exclaimed. "You're cheering me up and here I thought I was cheering you up!"

"You did?"

"It's why I told you the story of 144."

Khristen was silent. The story of the little tricolored heron did not seem to her a happy one.

Lola had found much to admire in the girl. The time and place was not of her making but whose time and place ever is? She'd be dealing with the rigors of the beyond soon enough.

She would discuss the Institute with her shortly. The Institute was *not* a suicide academy or a terrorist hospice. Or not exactly. Possibly the authorities would consider it so if they knew of its existence but they did not know of its existence. Its purpose was on another plane of comprehension entirely. To the extent that they were even aware of Lola, they considered her a harmless struggling businesswoman trying to make the best of a squat she'd taken over with an old friend of equal decrepitude, keeping up the

appearances of a simple-witted motel of yesteryear with plastic flowers in the window boxes, fishing poles for rent, and an absence of social networking or newsgathering devices for the few deluded travelers who thought they could get away for a few days from the reality of a permanently ongoing situation. Guests of the motel never advanced to the hotel. They weren't even aware of it, so determined were they to hold on to the old illusions. They were oblivious to the designs of the unseen oldsters and their extreme end-of-life plans. Had they been informed of such intentions they would have found them apocalyptical, though for all intents and purposes the apocalypse had pretty much occurred. The incomprehensible beauty of nature was no more, but most had accepted the destitution done in their name. It was over and now it could begin, was the way those on the outside justified their refreshed complacency. Lola's true tenantry were dedicated to disrupting that complacency.

Certainly no one expected the old to be difficult. The old were tolerable if they were reasonable and responsible enough to make way for the next ones, the new ones, the fresh ones, at their earliest opportunity. "Retirement communities" and "assisted living facilities" had long been in the process of being phased out as they no longer produced adequate profit to shareholders. The elderly were encouraged to depart life and they obliged with little protest and surprisingly few regrets. It had not been foreseen that some would turn on the very institutions that had made them the last beneficiaries of what was enshrined as progress. These oldsters, if not exactly a *force majeure,* were a baffling and bitter anomaly, characterized and dismissed as senile mavericks, lone termites or perfect examples of why the aged mind was not in the interests of society.

They did not consider themselves "terrorists," reserving that word for the bankers and builders, the industrial engineers, purveyors of war and the market, it goes without saying, the extermi-

nators and excavators, the breeders and consumers of every stripe, those locusts of clattering, clacking hunger.

When Lola's graduates reengaged with the world it was to make amends and instigate corrections, and not with fatuous good works either. They were given a directive, selected at random from a basket of folded papers. Some of the papers were worn and torn with handling and seemed destined never to be chosen.

There had been some successes, if tentative, when abruptly Lola found herself without her friend and soul traveler, Gordon. They had been reading Conrad together, Joseph Conrad, a favorite of theirs . . . *the last utterance will formulate, strange as it may appear, some hope now to us utterly inconceivable* . . . and they were just about to discuss this rather stygian statement when a largish lapse occurred. Gordon was no longer beside her though the book remained in her lap, the pages still turned to the old sailor's words. Since then, moments, months, however you cared to call them, had passed and Gordon had yet to appear. Even the collected works of Conrad went missing, not that she particularly wanted to consult them again. And she wouldn't be lying either if she said she harbored increasing reservations and misgivings about the current crop in residence. Khristen had arrived at a low point in the caliber of the place, certainly. Ideally, elderly people of purpose arrived, trained, meditated and were inspired, then went off to do their holy havoc but a logjam had gradually been building. The integrity of the Institute was at risk. Fewer people were getting through. Even the motel was seeing fewer visitors. In the past, guests would arrive determined to seize the simple pleasures of their yesterdays, pleasures so barely recalled that their reenactment could only be unsatisfactory. Burdened with an unhappiness greater even than they'd arrived with, they returned to a world they could only address with a refashioned and ruthless optimism. The birthday child and his mother were shaping up to be an exception to this, but to Lola's relief the two seemed no more awake to

the residents and purposes of the Institute than any of the other occasional guests.

The clouds had retreated with the sinking sun, and Big Girl resumed her avernal black. The long twilight commenced. Lola ate a few jelly beans and swallowed a Vicodin. She felt guilty about the Vicodin. She was just like anybody else, clinging on, thinking she'd have a thought she hadn't thought yet that would make all the difference. Twice she had taken mescaline. The first time she'd had an impression of absolute white, white beyond all whiteness. The second time there was blackness, a vivid all-encompassing black. She doubted a third time would have anything more to tell her.

She was losing nerve-cell population daily. Everyone was. The last physician she had gone to said it wasn't an acute problem. We have more nerve cells than we ever employ. Massive loss is not unacceptable, he assured her. He compared it to the amount of ink that can fade from a written message without changing what it says. She had found this charming. But there comes a moment when the message changes or becomes unintelligible or both, doesn't it, doctor? she had said. And he had smiled and said, Of course.

She considered once more the gaping dark that was Big Girl. Someone was down in her depths, this she'd once believed. A woman, of course, with long tangled hair. And all the wickedness of humankind against nature fell down through the waters and collected in her dark locks. Someone—shaman, vizier, gangrel— had to go down there and comb out her hair and confess and atone and promise, promise and atone and confess. This person would have to possess considerable authority and strength, certainly, to represent a desperate and repenting and lamenting people.

The old dear stories of possibility. No one wanted them anymore, but nothing had replaced them.

Jeffrey's birthday party was to take place at a bowling alley. When Khristen expressed surprise that amusements such as bowling alleys still existed, Lola said it was akin to the survival of lightbulbs lying intact on a rocky shore. Plus there was a little buffer zone around them here at the Institute where matters appeared to transpire in their customary nasty way, via establishments of entertainment mostly.

Thus Paradise Lanes flourished with its proud leagues, its rules and captains and hierarchical clubs. It was even expanding under new ownership to host children's birthday parties, which was highly controversial.

"I advised Barbara against going there but she said she was told that they provide balloons, pizza slices and cold drinks for the children as well as a mystery gift for the birthday child," Lola said. "All she has to pay for is the cake, the lanes and the adults' incidentals. It's the bowling leagues that's my concern, I know those people. That's a sacred place to them and Tuesday night their sacred hour. The new owner has no idea how seriously they take their traditions. They could make us feel most unwelcome. I foresee possible unpleasantness on a considerable scale, particularly if in the middle of it Barbara tells the boy that his father murdered his grandfather, which I think is her intention. They were a close-knit family until they unraveled. It happened at luncheon when little Jeffrey was at the dentist having his teeth cleaned. The men were arguing some legal technicality and it got out of hand. Mother and child have been fugitives from that fraught occurrence ever since."

"Does anybody know how to bowl?" Khristen asked.

Khristen sat in back with Jeffrey. He would be ten years old at seven o'clock that night. He held a boxed cake on his lap and stared through the cracked windshield of Lola's old car while maintaining a soft and running commentary with himself. ". . . now . . . similarly . . . unlike . . . objection . . . the point . . . the point is

well taken up to a point . . . may we justifiably harm one innocent in order to save the many? . . . objection . . . by the mutual agreement of parties concerned, all parties concerned . . . objection . . ."

"What does it feel like to be almost ten, Jeffrey?" Lola asked.

"What?" Jeffrey said.

"You're such a skinny little fellow. You must eat like a gerbil."

"I don't know what a gerbil eats."

"Oh, let's see, a gerbil eats ground nuts, beans, flaxseed oil maybe. Tea."

"If that's what my mother fed me she could be charged with assault, reckless endangerment and endangering the welfare of a child," Jeffrey said.

"You want to come up front and shift when I make my turn up here?" Lola inquired. "You push down, then over and down as I depress the clutch. You want to shift?"

"No, I don't," Jeffrey said. "Excuse me." He resumed his discouraging singsong. ". . . if the statute is content based, strict scrutiny applies . . . arbitrary and capricious . . . it is a well-established principle of statutory interpretation that the law favors rational and sensible construction . . ."

They pulled into the parking lot of Paradise Lanes and parked between a panel truck that had GOOD NEWS EXTERMINATING painted on the door and a sedan displaying a FORMER FETUS DRIVING sticker on the bumper.

"Frank Lloyd Wright designed this bowling alley," Lola informed them.

"Surely not!" Barbara protested. It was the first time she had spoken all evening.

"The blueprints suffered considerable compromises, though," Lola said. "The bowlers were locked in long and bitter conflict among themselves. Some of them had strokes."

"I'm sure that Frank Lloyd Wright would not for one moment have expended his talents on designing a bowling alley."

"In the beginning it was supposed to be on stilts," Lola said.

"Get out of the car, Jeffrey," Barbara said, breaking off this hopeless discussion. "Let's get this birthday over with. Don't look at that cake yet!"

He was dressed in a meticulous fashion: tasseled loafers, khaki pants, a white shirt and a seersucker jacket.

"I hope she doesn't let that cake do the talking for her," Lola said quietly to Khristen. "Like she'd re-create the murder scene in frosting and let him deduce the worst."

They followed mother and child into the building. The light inside was golden and the sound of falling pins relentless. The bowlers, men and women both, were of that pastime's typical bent—hefty, of a tribal disposition and with themselves well pleased. After they released the ball they held the afterward of their poses for a vanity of time.

"I want tickets for four," demanded Barbara of the concessionaire, "a gutter block, a pitcher of martinis, and a couple of chocolate milks. Forget the pizza and balloons."

"Is this the extent of the party?"

"That's right," Barbara said.

They were directed to the last lane, near the toilets, and seated at a small table there.

"Bowling's sort of like archery," Lola said to Jeffrey. "You want to hit the mark."

"Archery!" Barbara cried. "It couldn't be less like archery!"

"Shelley's Case," Jeffrey said worriedly. "I don't understand the definition of the rule in Shelley's Case. One of the first and most relevant cases in common law."

His mother looked at him disapprovingly. "Nobody has the capacity to understand the rule in Shelley's Case."

"That's right," the child said after a moment, clearly relieved. "Precedent, principle and policy. Everything depends upon the

choice made from a large number of possible broader propositions."

"Before he discovered the verbal wiles of the law he had to use an inhaler," Barbara said to Lola.

"Do you know what civil death is, Jeffrey?" Lola asked.

"The deprivation of civil rights as a result of being declared an outlaw," little Jeffrey said happily.

"The kid cannot be stumped. Nothing stumps him," Barbara said.

The beverages arrived as well as the mystery gift, which proved to be a paper bag containing a buzzer ring, a plastic fly in a plastic ice cube and a splash of authentic-looking vomit, also plastic.

"Well would you look at that, Jeffrey," Lola said. "Some care went into this selection for a little boy."

"I don't want to bowl, Mother," Jeffrey said.

"Of course not. Of course you don't. It's out of the question."

"Potential autonomy is insufficient to prove," Jeffrey crooned softly. "Objection! . . . hypothetical and speculative . . ."

"You're going to be a great barrister," Barbara said, savoring the last of the pitcher of martinis. "Nothing will prevent it from happening, neither the loss of our fortune nor the dignity of our family name."

"Hey, Lane Fifteen," a woman yelled. "You gonna bowl? People come here to bowl. Show some respect." She and her group wore bright orange sateen jackets with GOOD NEWS EXTERMINATING whorling in thick red thread upon the back.

"We need plates and forks," Barbara said. "I'll get them." But when she returned she bore only another pitcher of martinis.

"Do you ever," Lola asked, "after a few cocktails see everything as being tiny? Everything exceptionally tiny? Lilliputian even?"

"No," Barbara said.

"You're almost afraid to touch anything for fear you'll crush it, without meaning to."

"No."

"Because that's characteristic of raging alcoholism."

"Having a drink in a tiny house with tiny things scattered about would be quite disturbing," Barbara conceded.

"Could we cut the cake now?" Jeffrey asked. Khristen was surprised he directed the question to her. She could not recall a single birthday, not one.

The words hung recklessly in the air. "Yes," Barbara said. "It's time. Happy Birthday, darling. I may not have handled everything as well as I could have."

With her long fingernails, Barbara slit the tape that secured the flaps of the box, closed her eyes and shoved back the lid.

A disturbing scene was disclosed, executed in frosting.

"Daddy's dead," Jeffrey said.

Barbara's eyes flipped open. "I knew the baker wouldn't do this right! What a goddamn backwater this place is! I described the situation as I had witnessed it in the same way I described it to the police who complimented me at the time on my lucidity and calm. I had certainly made their work easier, they told me. And this baker assured me he grasped the situation. He had been in the armed forces, he told me, and had seen mayhem, he had seen the results of disagreement. He was also sensitive to the subtleties of disclosure, he told me, and yet look at this . . . he reversed every-thing! He mixed everything up!"

"I was wondering where you located a baker," Lola said.

"Who was I speaking to if not a baker!" Barbara demanded.

"Daddy's not dead?" Jeffrey said.

"Your goddamn father is alive but he's in big trouble this time."

"You never liked Daddy," Jeffrey mused. "You should have obtained a divorce years ago, before I was born even."

"Could it be someone else's cake order?" Khristen suggested,

although this seemed unlikely. "It's not very nice, is it? Maybe it tastes better than it looks."

"Most people around here bake their own cakes when the fancy strikes them which isn't often," Lola persisted.

"Is it me who's dead?" Jeffrey asked.

"Don't be willfully dense, darling. Give Mother a bit of a break here."

"I'm merely curious."

"Don't be," his mother snapped. "It's a characteristic worthless in a lawyer." She pitched the false fly in the false ice cube into the empty pitcher.

"What I really wanted for my birthday was a mock-up of a jury box in my bedroom," Jeffrey confided to Khristen. "Perhaps it will be there upon our return."

"Who would be in the jury box?" Khristen asked.

"I have very few friends. I suppose there wouldn't be anyone there."

"You, yo! Lane Fifteen!" the woman bawled.

"That damn baker just copied *Saturno* on the cake," Barbara complained.

"Can't miss that," Lola agreed. To Khristen she said, "A very famous and disturbing painting by the Spaniard, Goya. I can see why the baker might consider it but in the case of little Jeffrey here and his father and grandfather, the situation is the opposite."

"You! Loiterers!" the woman called. "No loitering here."

"One more minute and I'm going to take her personalized bowling ball and cram it down her throat," Barbara said. She looked alarmingly bright-eyed.

Jeffrey was studying the cake. The background frosting was blue and looked thoroughly toxic. He did not wear glasses but if recalled by others he was a frail little boy in large smudged glasses.

"The painting is actually called *Saturn Devouring His Son*,"

Lola whispered to Khristen, "though it could just as well be his daughter."

Khristen nodded. It was a helpless, naked human figure. Gender played no part.

"The important thing to know—no, to *realize*—is that Saturn, whenever and however depicted, represents Time, which, with its ravenous appetite for life, devours all its creations, whether they are beings, things, ideas or sentiments," Lola said.

How remarkable it was, Khristen thought, to be able to discourse on fine art in a bowling alley where you were not welcome.

"Whoever made this cake did a pretty good job considering the crudity of the decorating caps available now for affixing to the frosting tubes," Lola continued. " 'Course we never will know who it was made this cake."

"It's seven o'clock, darling," Barbara said to Jeffrey. "You've just left the first decade of your life behind. You're a little man now."

"I'm not. I'm a minor. I have years before I'm *sui juris*. Surely you know that, Mother."

"A threshold has been passed," Barbara insisted.

A muscular fellow in a tight T-shirt was approaching them.

"Perhaps we should leave," murmured Lola. The shirt had a question imprinted upon it. GOT SAND? He stood before them, shaking his head.

"What is he, mute?" Barbara asked.

"You about through here?" the man inquired. "We got people requesting this lane. This is a desirable lane."

"What does that mean?" Jeffrey asked.

"It means there's people want to bowl where you're not bowling."

"I'm referring to your shirt, 'Got sand?' What does that mean?"

"It means he's a laborer, Jeffrey," Barbara said, stifling a hic-

cup. "All these people here are probably laborers of some sort, working with their hands, leveling and paving or some such goddamned backwater thing."

"Sand means grit, courage, backbone," the man said, enraged. "Fools, it means *cojones*."

"*Cojones!*" Barbara exclaimed. "Oh please." She belched.

"I don't under . . ." Jeffrey began.

The man's annoyed gaze fell on the grimly colorful cake in its snowy box. "God in heaven," he said, stepping back.

"Jeffrey, honey, we are going to help your mother up. She needs some assistance. Khristen, dear, you bring that cake. We're leaving right now, mister."

Khristen rather expected the night to be pleasant after the atmosphere of the bowling alley but there was a seared, sad smell to it, a smell she had familiarized herself with, she guessed, but was still capable of forgetting.

Barbara clung to the door handle of Lola's car. "Yes, you're a little man now, Jeffrey. I should tell you about the night you were born sometime."

"It shall be unlawful for any person to promote, advertise, stage, hold, manage, conduct, participate in, engage in or carry on . . ." Jeffrey recited sternly. "What . . . oh no, Mother, thank you, you need not."

"You were so small and precious. I was afraid to touch you. All your little bones, you know? And hair, you had so much hair . . . I never wanted another one after you, that's for sure. I would never, never, never go through something like that again."

"Mother?"

"I've got a long birth canal. My birth canal's too long. It was such hell. I barely survived."

"Mother?"

"Yes, darling."

"Would it be permissible to throw away the cake?"

"The cake? Certainly. Horrid cake. No help at all."

"Perhaps the animals in the woods might eat it," Jeffrey said.

"There aren't any animals in these woods," Lola said, "not even those chimps who were brought to be saved. Our native sons have pretty much shot everything out. There was a chimp retreat a few miles from here not that long ago, you know, one of those chimp retirement homes for those who so faithfully served in space shots and non-mutilating experiments and such. The idea was that these aged chimps would have their own fenced-in retreat of a few hundred acres and caring people would provide them with dog kibble and fresh water daily and the chimps would spend their final days climbing trees and drawing pictures in the dirt with sticks and eating apricots. It had the potential of becoming a tourist attraction, one of those offbeat ones some people are keen to discover. Those chimps would gaze at you with such cold resentment—no empathy at all, no gratitude either—and a lot of folks got quite a kick out of that. But some good old boys snuck in one Saturday night and picked off those chimps one by one like they were squirrels, shot them right out of the trees they were living in. They even shot Betty. She was the one used to bathe her baby dolls in the washtub."

This must be the past, the past, Khristen thought.

"That would be punishable by . . ." Jeffrey began, but then fell silent.

"Before the eyes can see, they must be incapable of tears," Khristen said.

"I've heard that too and I certainly aspire to it," Lola said. "But when I heard they murdered Betty, I just bawled."

Jeffrey's milestone party could hardly have been considered a success, but he and his mother remained in residence at the motel.

"She might still be trying to explain that cake to him," Lola said to Khristen. "Plus nobody likes commencing a journey of return in the rain."

Indeed, rain was pouring off the roof and leaving nasty bubbles in the puddled dirt. It was twisting inside, too, in a slender stream to collapse in a large bucket that had once held chlorine tablets.

## ⚠ *AVISO* ⚠

"They expect it to continue through the weekend with all next week promising to be oppressive," Lola said.

Big Girl was invisible. Lola said that in all the time she'd been here she had never seen the lake accept a single drop that fell from the sky.

They were in the big building's lobby, watching the stuff come down. An elderly man was standing before them, just outside the windows, shoeless and shirtless with his arms and head flung back.

"He's going to drown like a turkey someday doing that," Lola said. "I don't allow my bird of paradise out in it and there he is, gulping it down."

The plant's sipping water was drawn through cheesecloth, boiled then cooled. The bird of paradise was the one thing Lola coddled and still it did not look healthy.

She dragged the half-full bucket to the window and dashed the contents outside.

She and Khristen stared together at the ugly rain falling and the figure Lola called Hector standing at limp attention in it.

"He's going to get yaws or worse," Lola said.

The rain gifted a pink light to the so-called day, a light that irradiated every hair on Lola's head. Khristen could have counted them and finished with an accurate number and it wouldn't have taken her long.

Lola opened the door and shouted, "Go inside, fool!"

"It's filling the aquifers," the fright that was Hector cried. "It's filling the aquifers of this land."

"That stuff's not filling aquifers and you know it. The aquifers are collapsed."

Hector shook his head, then his whole self, like a dog, but the rain did not fly off him in pleasant droplets as it would from a dog. It clung grayly like tiny sticky-bodied caterpillars to his skin.

"He's courting pneumonia or some other pulmonary event," Lola said. "That's what they used to call the old person's friend, pneumonia. Some friend. Like having a three-hundred-pound officer of the law sitting on your chest advising you that it's not in your best interests to draw that next breath."

Hector waded toward them across a hard pan remarkably resistant to percolation and sidled into the room, his skin mottled like an unripe strawberry.

"You'd better rub yourself down with vinegar or the itching's going to be terrible."

"Which came first in your opinion, Lola, the rabid rain or the birdless dawn?" Hector stared at Khristen.

"All I know is that the rain changed her nature some fourteen months ago," Lola said.

"Fourteen is a marvelous number! One philosopher even goes so far as to say that it is impossible for fourteen minutes to pass. Something about it corresponding to infinity. Oh, I used to study these things! This philosopher was greatly influenced by an earlier philosopher he had misunderstood completely. This is how all great discoveries arise, through misunderstanding. Could you locate that vinegar for me? Do you really think vinegar would help?"

"I know it's here or certainly was," Lola said.

"I just wanted to take a simple pleasure of feeling falling rain," Hector said. He looked about to cry.

"Rain's not rain if it's not falling," Lola said mildly.

He squinted at Khristen. "Who is she," he demanded of Lola. "She's like someone."

"You go on now, Hector, take this towel." She extended a beach towel, faded almost to transparency, a skeletal palm and ghostly coconuts.

"Oh, I like this one," he said, draping it with a flourish around his bones.

After he left, Lola threw the contents of another brimming bucket outside. The stuff hit the ground as limply as a body might. Khristen almost expected it to coalesce into something like an eel and swing jerkily out of sight.

"I remember when it fell so pretty, sparkling, and the smell, with no exaggeration, was divine." Lola sighed. "The Institute's winding down. Just the dotty ones are left or those whose abilities have greatly diminished. Scarlett was supposed to shiv an herbicide representative but is dragging her heels, Tom had planned on going to a trophy-hunting convention and poisoning all there including the children with their tyke-sized AK-47's but he's been beset with sudden blindness and will have to find another way to implement. No one wants to leave anymore. They're worrying about what comes next again."

"I won't stay," Khristen assured her.

"Oh I'm not referring to you, dear. This is no determinant for you. I've always believed that there are seven epochs in each person's life. They proceed like seasons. There's spring, late spring, early summer, summer, fall and winter." She grinned at Khristen. "That's just six, you're about to say. Winter counts twice as well, but I think you've blown right through the winter phases. So much has to be recalibrated. There's a thirteenth constellation now so

even the zodiac has to be reconsidered. *Ophiuchus.* That's the new one. No one wants to be born under it."

There was a metal rack for postcards in the office which Khristen nudged into motion.

"No one wants to get through to this place either. It's because they don't believe in absolution, and you know why? Because absolution for what has been done is impossible. I used to try to recruit, it's true, make the place more thrivey but no more. If circumstances bring a person to comprehension they'll find the gate."

"I don't remember a gate," Khristen said.

"It swings out and it swings in though it can scarcely be called a gate anymore, it's in such darkened disrepair, resulting in the errancy, I'm sure, of little Jeffrey and his mother. But whenever mistakes like that happen, I try to present the illusion as best I can and in the most discreet manner. I steer them away to the motel. Show them the beach and the wickets, the balls and the tackle. Show them the gaming gallery and the pool and the wrought-iron tables where they can enjoy their toast. Show them where the clean linens are kept. Yet, you know, even with all the effort expended upon those who aren't even supposed to be here, I've heard more than once *I'm so bored I could die . . .*"

Suddenly she broke off. "How is your room?" she inquired. "What room did I give you again?"

"Room Five. Opposite Honey, Heart of Gold."

Khristen had not yet seen Honey, nor anyone else in the immense, listing building. Yet it only appeared deserted, Lola had told her. There were more than a dozen in residence, possibly fourteen—that perfect and impossible number—but Lola was so bad with figures it was anyone's guess. One resident had left not long before Khristen's arrival with the intention of blowing himself up in the middle of one of those thousand-acre truck and bulldozer dealerships that were so popular. And he *had* succeeded

in blowing himself up, causing some cosmetic damage to a few of the machines but the days were long past when an event like that would give anyone pause, to say nothing of bestirring greater consciousness. She compared his burning to a gummy bear on fire, one of those candies. It had meant no more than that, Death having lost her bump.

"Oh yes. How is Room Five?"

Khristen admitted she couldn't remember it. It had been just the night before after all. But to describe it she would have to imagine it now and what if she hurt Lola's feelings? She liked Lola so much. She would like to lay her head on her speckled breast, on her warm and tragic bosom.

She gently pushed at the revolving rack again. "Do you have any other cards I could put in here? You're all out except for the dining room." She supposed the more interesting ones had been selected long before.

"I've been all out save for the dining room for some while," Lola said.

"What were the other cards you used to have?"

"We had one of a pie with accompanying list of ingredients and directions I hear was popular."

"Which of these two is the better seller? The one with the room full of people or the one with the room empty? That room's not even here anymore, is it?"

"Fire before my time. But you can see there were once considerable banquet facilities. And any number of lecture halls and such."

Khristen held a card displaying the room empty. The colors were faded, the linens draping the four long receding trestle tables were gray, the squatty glow of the many lamps a wan yellow. Still, everything was in order, each setting the same, every chair identical to the one beside it. And then, there was the other one, the long room full, every seat taken.

"They were all kind of obedient, weren't they," Khristen noted. "All looking in the same direction. There must have been speakers, presentations."

"There's a Latin phrase for that sort of business," Lola said. "Those people had a phrase for pretty much everything, it turns out. In this case, *festum stultorum*. Fools' feast. I used to think that there's more people alive at present than all the people who ever lived and that's why we all feel so strange and everything's not right. But the fact is that those of us who are alive today are only 5.5 percent of all the people who ever lived. But you know me and numbers. I may be off by a bit."

"And that's probably why we feel so strange and nothing's right," Khristen said.

Despite Lola's prediction, the rain withdrew. Khristen went outside and walked, counting her steps at first and then not counting. The steaming earth tugged at her, the wind snapped. She thought, This is still a day, it's still called a day. Below a yellowed rise, the motel appeared in shy certitude. She saw Jeffrey pacing before it.

"Legal fictions," he was saying. "A legal fiction has allowed the court to attribute legal personhood not just to autonomous non-conscious nonsentient humans but to trusts, corporations, religious idols and ships."

"Hi, Jeffrey."

He paused and looked at her. "I'm going to be a judge, you know."

"Why not," she said agreeably.

"Are you an inhabitant of here or there? My mother says you give her the creeps."

Khristen laughed.

"It's not a laughing matter, you know. Very little is. Still, you're correct in dismissing her opinion of you. It's my opinion of you that matters and I haven't formed one yet. I find you . . .

opaque. Of course the whole situation is opaque. I expected more incandescence. But I'm just a child. I'm naive in many ways."

"Jeffrey!" his mother called from a plaid lounger. "Get over here this minute!"

"My mother . . ." he began, ". . . should be viewed in these circumstances much as the post-disaster present should be understood in relation to the pre-disaster past. She is behaving unsympathetically and without a shred of compassion or consideration but . . ."

"Jeffrey! Get your bottom over here now!"

Jeffrey sighed. "Excuse me a sec." He trotted off, giving the huge inflatable swan that occupied most of the pool a smack as he passed. Barbara had managed to bring it along under what must have been decidedly difficult conditions. There was the pleasant archaic smell of tanning oil in the air.

"I have a question," he said when he returned. "What was your favoritemost thing out there?"

"Out where?"

"Favoritemost." He smacked his forehead. "Good heavens, it's so easy to regress."

"You needn't regress with me."

"Why not? You have the blank expectancy of an extremely young individual. Are you familiar with the works of Kierkegaard?"

"In school. A bit. Very much in passing," Khristen confessed.

"He pathetically wanted the words 'The Individual' etched upon his gravestone but that didn't happen. So little of what we— actors before an anonymous public—hope for in this life actually occurs," Jeffrey said darkly. "What was carved on his stone was a scrap of a sentimental hymn. I recall but a bit of it: *Then the whole struggle entirely disappears*. It makes me nauseous to remember the rest."

"The leap of faith is what we learned," Khristen said.

"Well I would certainly hope so. He also wanted to work cata-

strophically in the last days of his life but I believe that wish was denied him as well."

"What's it like to work catastrophically, do you think?"

"It's what the nutcases here are trying to do but you would know better than I."

"I've come across only a few people here. The place seems pretty empty."

"On the contrary, it's teeming. Mother thinks it's a riot."

"Did anyone offer to give you a tour?"

"We certainly would not subject ourselves to a tour," Jeffrey said. "We've never taken a tour in our lives. But I heard Lola suggest that you give them tours in that colorful vehicle you arrived in."

"She hasn't mentioned it again."

"I suppose you would need a script."

"I suppose. I don't know the area, I haven't explored it much. I haven't even made a circuit around the lake."

"Oh my goodness," he said. "Everyone does that. I've seen dozens do that."

"So you've walked around the lake?"

"No," he said. "That would be quite impossible." He added, "Mother would never allow it." He pointed to his shoes which were new, white and vaguely preposterous. "When we first arrived Lola attempted to interest me in the lake after being informed of my interest in maritime law. She calls her Big Girl, you know. And she says the nice thing about Big Girl is that if you concentrate, she eventually notices you. She's very much sunk into her own thoughts, is Lola's understanding of the lake, but just possibly, you might be accepted as a figure of interest by Big Girl and in that moment you become real, you can feel yourself being real."

"Oh that's lovely," Khristen exclaimed. "Lola is so kind."

Jeffrey looked at her wanly. "Which is the exact opposite of

what occurs when one tries to gain the attention of the Sphinx. I doubt you've been to Egypt?"

"I haven't been to Egypt."

"My grandfather took me there when I was seven. None of this European nonsense—London, Rome, Paris. Those places were of no interest to my tata and therefore to me. We went to see the Sphinx and I had exactly the experience my tata said I would have. The Sphinx does not look at you and you cannot possibly catch its gaze. It looks past, past, past into the distances of eternity. It doesn't see you. It's not that you are merely insignificant, you are too transient. Your transience is so great that you do not exist."

Ants were crawling over Jeffrey's magnificent shoes in operatic urgency.

"Beings such as ourselves could not have created the Sphinx," he concluded.

"Jeffrey!" his mother screamed. "Did you put the wafer for the ice machine in your pocket again!"

"It's not a wafer, Mother, it's a token, a counterfeit coin as it were."

"Well it's never where it's supposed to be!"

Jeffrey put one hand in his pocket and frowned.

"Must go," he said to Khristen.

The next time Khristen entered the office, the rack holding the postcards was gone. As was the bird of paradise. The ⚠ *AVISO* ⚠ buckets were stacked haphazardly in a corner.

"Would you do me a favor, dear?" Lola asked.

Would Khristen visit James in Room Thirty-Three and inform him that Frick was dead?

"Who is Frick?"

"He experimented on animals, dear, up to the very end of his

days. His chain of vivisection labs was one of the few corporations that survived even this most recent disaster. Injecting drugs, diseases, poisons into animals was his life's affirming career. Human beings are autonomous, everything else is not, was his belief and it afforded him great latitudes of cruelty."

"How was James going to stop him?"

"Originally he planned on kidnapping him and bringing him back here for reprogramming but the logistics proved impossible. James fancied himself a psychologist though I believe he once worked in some maritime industry. But even if he were a psychologist or there was a psychologist among us here and Frick was convinced to renounce his life in service, a life devoted to shocking, blinding, sickening and maiming thousands of animals, a career built on the countless limbs unnecessarily amputated, the brains ablated, skulls trephined, even if Frick reached the clarity of utterly realizing the wickedness of his generously funded unethical and repetitive experiments and was articulate in expressing his remorse and new awareness, he would no longer be speaking the language of those who had previously understood him. His words would not be understood. And what would the vivisectionist's transformation of mind accomplish anyway? Where is the gain in the transformation of heart of a single person?

"James gave up on reprogramming. He worked on the way of balance for a while, the way of peace, but that was a nonstarter. I think he just went back to wanting him dead. Frick being dead doesn't let either one of them off the hook of course but it might give James some relief. He's been working on that bastard for ever so long. Now if you find that James is dead himself, which is not unlikely, you just come back and get me. Is this too much to ask?" She seemed to consider this.

"No, that's all right," Khristen said.

"It might be too much to ask. He's so old," Lola added. "He's on oxygen."

Khristen climbed the crumbling staircases. The iron railings were rusted, pitted in parts like lace. Each door had a faint number etched into the wood. She knocked, and after several moments of silence, knocked again.

The room was painted purple, a softly pulsating purple. There was no furniture, not even a rug on the floor but on one wall dozens of photographs of people were posted, some with X's inked upon them. They were not unsmiling state-issued IDs but glossy formal portraits.

"Hello! Mr. James?"

There was no reply but in the corner furthest from the light that struggled through the dirty window, crouched in a niche like Diogenes in his tub, was a pile of rags, which stirred. Two arms emerged, transparent as the wings of certain insects, then a bearded face.

"Is he dead?"

"Lola told me to tell you that Frick is dead," Khristen reported.

"It worked!" the wizened creature cried weakly. "Did he suffer terribly?"

"I don't think so," for Lola had told her that he died at his home, age ninety-two, revered by his sons and daughters, his grandsons and granddaughters and generations of students.

But James was making such a racket lowering himself from his niche, she doubted that he had heard her. He staggered over to the wall of photographs, leaving behind an oxygen tank of bilious green scratched in many places.

"I feel I've turned the corner now! Oh some of the devils have died all right but in their own sweet time." He had reached the wall and with a filthy finger made a serviceable X across the smiling likeness of a stout man in a tuxedo. "Tell me everything, whoever you are, divine herald. Did he have to be restrained in his agony? Did he scream to dog's god for mercy? Oh I was feeling the gift with that fucking Frick. I was focused, I was feeding him dread.

I attribute it to the purple. I recently repainted the walls, do you see, and I knew the instant I was finished I had him. It was a knife blade of energy that penetrated his filthy heart. It's a powerful color, perfectly in accord with my purposes. Virgil said it was the color of the soul. Do you know who invented the soul? Pindar. A Greek. Centuries before."

Invented, Khristen marveled.

"See these devils here, see them," he said, stabbing his finger at another photograph of two men in lab coats, "do you know who they are?"

"You've crossed them out."

He pushed a button on the wall and a strong young voice issued forth.

"Two behavioral scientists who specialized in introducing psychopathology in primates. They began by raising infant monkeys in stainless steel chambers with no contact with any other living thing, thus inducing irreversible mental illness. They'd gotten a few papers out of it. But then they wanted to go beyond raising them with no mothers, they wanted to see what would happen if they provided them with puppet mothers made of hair and cloth, monster mothers who would erratically and without warning eject brass darts or high-pressure compressed air that would blow the infants' skin practically off their bodies."

"When did this happen!" Khristen cried.

The voice continued. "Then, and they felt this was only logical, they wanted to observe what would occur if the monkeys that survived bore offspring. In accordance with evolving refinements in isolation, one of them devised a rack for impregnation purposes, the 'rape rack.' When the infants were born, the mothers, according to the researchers' reports, attacked them in the most sickening manner, throttling and biting their bodies, crushing their skulls. They found it interesting how the legendary mothering instinct could be so systematically eliminated. They got a few

more papers out of this and then retired. Relearning more appropriate behaviors was a project for others to explore."

With a broken black fingernail he pushed the button again and the voice ceased.

"They moved to Truth or Consequences, New Mexico, and opened a B&B there," he croaked. "*Singing Winds Bed and Breakfast.* They devoted themselves to plumping pillows, baking popovers, oiling the fowling guns. They remained impervious to my most concentrated efforts. I projected pain and more pain upon them and all that happened was the further deterioration and decay of my own self. I made myself sick while they enjoyed good health and happiness. They died when their turquoise convertible failed to negotiate a curve. They died instantly, untroubled, untouched by my efforts whereas it took me weeks to leave the experimental chamber in my mind that I'd placed them in."

He scratched at the complacent face in Frick's photograph until a disc of purple wall appeared.

"Tell me. Details. I see him grotesquely bloated like the dogs he poisoned," he said faintly.

He looked at her uneasily. Perhaps she was no divine herald after all, no star-born one, no ethereal being sent to aid him. She was raggedy-looking, sinewy, a shy brown bird, not that that would disqualify her of course, but she might well not be his assuring angel.

"I used to have the animals on these walls before the walls were purple. The animal subjects. I gazed at them day and night. I tried to inhabit them, heal them, transform them. Evil is not real, it is destructible and can be converted. It is good that it is indestructible. That's what I sobbed morning and evening but it was all junk. It went out of my heart as junk and it brought back junk. My attempts to engage with their poor tortured selves failed, so I moved on to pictures of their executioners."

From the considerable dust wadded against the floorboards,

James pulled another photograph and pressed it against the wall. It was a woman surrounded by a group of little girls in Brownie uniforms, an informal shot taken by an undercover operative who had subsequently been arrested. It was the best the poor fellow could do, he could never get near her workplace, he was only able to track her down at a Brownie jamboree where she was volunteering. The Brownies were absolutely clueless as to her profession, the details of which had been scrubbed for their tiny ears. Miss Smith worked with animals, is what those little ears heard. The woman held several doctorates and had been going through her subjects like popcorn for decades. Maybe she was dead now, too, with a memorial plaque and a funded wing somewhere, no longer briskly crazing capuchin monkeys and severing the spines of hounds.

He didn't feel good. He had never felt less well, actually. "When I first got here I felt great despair," he admitted, "despair and disgust. I longed for confrontation, revenge. Through acts of revenge would come awakening. That was my belief. But my thinking just bounced off their evil like a ball from a wall. And then another deeper comprehension arose. These deliberately poisoned and maimed animals are one with the tortured savior. Both suffer so man can ultimately be saved. And it never ends. But no matter! The tomb is never empty. The tomb is forever full. Immanence is everywhere."

She looked so sad, this figure before him, why did she look so sad?

"It's been some time since I had a visitor," he said. "I was beginning to think that everyone had jumped ship, so to speak. Lola lacks managerial ability, she needs more staff."

He squinted at her but she didn't seem to be speaking. Had she been speaking? *Even though you are alone in a dark room conduct yourself as though you were facing a noble guest.* Naturally easier to

do when no one was there. And not to be unkind, but this one appeared to be no noble guest.

"I kept the photographs of course. I didn't throw them away." He rubbed his chest through the worn cloth of his shirt, feeling the plastic bag taped there. Beneath it his skin was inflamed, festering. The animals were here, close to his heart but beyond his or anyone's ministrations. There was a dog, sitting in a chair, an old office chair with a swivel seat. There was grass beneath the chair and a cement wall with a louvered window behind it, the photograph was gray and white, the dog was spotted. The chair had been rolled out into the yard on its rubber casters. Or perhaps it was always out there. Perhaps this was where they took the pictures before . . . before what? Their work was done. The subject had been fed drugs to induce cirrhosis of the liver. Human hands held his forelegs extended, keeping the grotesquely bloated body erect. He was thus tall as a child, a child of ten perhaps, a child to whom evil had been incomprehensibly administered by some cruel *erlking*.

Had she left? She was so quiet. No. She was extending her hand to his, patting his lightly. He recoiled.

"Wonder, the seed of knowledge. You shock it and see . . . You kill it and see . . ." he muttered. "It never ends."

Was that the door stumbling shut once more? Someone had been there certainly. But now, no.

He turned to his niche. He was weary, he was done. He caressed the old green tank. It was filled with helium, for a moment just like this one, for once effort ceases in life, the movement is downward. This has been known since remote times.

Lola thought it was oxygen, something to keep him going, keep him enlisted, but she didn't know! Nor would the body know. To the body, helium was perfectly fine, one breath as good as another. The brain was already in on the game, the heart the last to know, poor heart.

He pulled the scuffed, cool tank closer and straightened its waxy tubes. It was the same color as his old thermos on the trawler. Sometimes it held coffee, but mostly whiskey. It kept him going, and for many years what a gay science it had been, the work he'd done, scouring the seabed clean, sucking the eminence from those proud depths.

Hard work but they had done it. It had taken years, but he and his crew had done it.

He tore the bag of pictures from his chest and patted it for a moment, then clipped the tubes to his dry nostrils, twisted a dial and pulled the bag over his head. It smelled of dust and his own long stink. Thoughts moved slowly through his head like a procession of starving animals. They seemed to be taking the place of his breaths. But the animals disappeared one by one, and then the procession ended.

No one had ever popped off on the grounds of the Institute before, it was deeply unprecedented. Lola didn't even know how to dispose of the body. She liked the tradition of the *dakhma*—the Towers of Silence—but there weren't any vultures anymore. It was the vultures that were essential to the Towers of Silence. But James weighed no more than an armful of twigs which the remains indeed resembled. Whatever problem inherent in their further disintegration would resolve itself.

Now Lola and Khristen were painting the walls of his old room with tubs of gray, of which there seemed to be an inexhaustible supply.

"He had no business slapping on that lurid color," Lola complained. "Where on earth did he find such a purple? He was probably trying to pattern himself on the desert fathers but went off course. Not that they were actual fathers, they were all sterile as mules, but they'd go into the desert as solitaries and grapple with

the devil. Some contend that they saved civilization which had been pretty much reduced to empty ceremony, execution and bell ringing at a very crucial time.

"Civilization," Khristen said thoughtfully.

"They saved it by denying it with vicious certitude," Lola said. "But my point is that they wrestled with the devil. There were no lavender walls and oxygen provided, that's for sure."

Khristen tried to picture the desert fathers. They were toothless and glorious, lunging through black sands, preaching to the dung beetles and confronting the devil whenever feasible. When they died, lions, weeping, dug the graves with their great claws.

"When they were grappling with the devil were they wrestling with evil? Is it the same thing?"

"No! That's the mistake that was made from the get-go. Those two are only distantly related. You can beat the devil and not hobble evil one bit. We've locked up the devil with his mirrors and peacocks and let the real felon free. The devil's nothing more than evil's colorful distraction, his myth, his clown. Evil made the devil just like God made little Jesus and for the same incomprehensible ends."

Khristen looked at the paint congealing in the bristles of the brush. The brush wasn't working right. She lay it down on a piece of newspaper, an obituary page, and had a stinging recollection of her father's funeral day, when she'd been commanded to imagine the dead child's future.

Lola extended a paint-gummed finger toward a stripling's goofy stance. He was wearing a bola tie.

"That one died during the bad hamburger epidemic. This paper is so old. Of course they don't publish anymore. People don't bother with obituaries. They're a thing of the past."

"Bad hamburger," Khristen said. It sounded like a pet being scolded.

"It was at one of those big Harvest Festivals. Many sickened,

some succumbed. It turned out—well this was only one of the facts disclosed—that a single patty, they call them patties for some reason, can contain the flesh of a hundred animals. This disturbed some people. They wanted their food to be more singular."

"I'm supposed to know what happens when you die," Khristen said. "I was told so."

"You're still worrying that little baby-step death of yours! Well you shouldn't. You can't rely on your own experience in that instance. It's just a theory. The Hindus have an elaborate theory for example. With the Hindus when you die you leave Hinduland and go to heaven. You find that all your enemies are there whereas all your loved ones are in hell. This is not as terrible as it appears to be for all you have to do is have the wit to say, 'Why I prefer to stay in the blackness and horror of hell with my dear ones for where they are is heaven to me,' and immediately both heaven and hell vanish. All appearances vanish. You pass beyond them. And you're in a perfect state of being where there's nothing that's not its exact opposite. I forget the name they give it. It's supposed to be wonderful. You're supposed to achieve this before you die, though definitely your last chance is right after, immediately after."

"You just say 'I want to stay with my loved ones' and they vanish, too, along with the blackness and the horror?" Khristen said doubtfully.

"It's not anything you could possibly want which is possibly the point of it."

"What happens if you don't think to say it?"

"Think to say what, dear?"

"If you figure that's the way it's going to be and always was—that you end up in heaven with your enemies or in hell with those you loved?"

"Oh!" Lola said. "Then you're just stuck until the next time

around. That is not supposed to be desirable. Now don't hide that brush away so I'll think I've misplaced it," and she began gathering up the rags and paints and papers. "That gray covered better than I expected. It's a most forgiving color. Are you feeling all right, dear? We've probably been in this stuffy space too long. When we're done, which I declare we are, I'm not going to utilize this room again. I'll put a padlock on the door big as a horse's eye. One of my very good friends—oh this was long ago—opined that eternity was a forgotten horse. I liked that so much that I wanted to think eternity was a forgotten horse, too, but she said that wasn't fair. I've never been able to come up with anything half that good."

"So lonely," Khristen said. She did not like the image of eternity being a forgotten horse.

"Lonely's the name of the game, my dear. I'm going over to the motel now with some supplies. Would you care to accompany me? I've never seen anybody go through glasses the way Barbara does. I think she forgets where she put them."

Together they descended the sagging steps. From the office Lola retrieved a box in which there were several clean and similar glasses, though they were more like jars.

Jeffrey was standing on the sodden lawn with a large book in his hands.

". . . strict construction, textualism, living constitutionalism . . ." He looked up at them, blinking.

"How is your mother? What's she doing today?" Lola inquired.

"Resting," Jeffrey said, returning to the tome. ". . . original intent can also be a building block of any interpretative theory . . ." He raised one small hand dramatically, forestalling interruption. ". . . though of course one must also address ambiguity and textual silence."

"I'll just put the glasses she requested down here," Lola said.

Back in the office which offered its usual powerful bouquet of

mildew, Khristen said, "Do you think people write books to create havoc or for some other reason?"

Lola dismissed this query about an author's intentions as all but unanswerable.

They stood in silence for a time. Nothing stirred.

"I miss the animals," Khristen said.

"Ah yes, people always seemed to resent them so."

"I used to think that animals could be immortal because they were innocent of death."

"Whoever told you that!" Lola exclaimed. "That's a doozy. There's nothing that ignorant."

"They're immortal and that's why they don't live with us anymore. It was something, given the circumstances, I figured out for myself. But I was very little then, young."

"That's a different matter then," Lola relented. "A lovely thought," she conceded. "Much nicer than that fellow around Darwin's time—can't remember his name—a respected scientist, a vulcanologist he was, and his belief was that animals become extinct because God stops thinking about them. You would think people would find the notion quite alarming but it found favor in many circles. It's actually back in fashion again."

Khristen looked uncertainly about the office which seemed even more cramped with nothing in it but the ⚠ *AVISO* ⚠ buckets and a rusting multidrawer filing cabinet.

"Where is your plant?" she asked.

"I stopped thinking about it," Lola said. "Haha! Oh, I'm sorry, dear. Forgive me. Everything has become so . . . unwieldy. Would you do me another favor, dear? Would you help me a bit with Scarlett? She's delaying her exit again. Perhaps you could try and re-enthuse her about her project."

"What is her project?"

"The plan was to wipe out a number of people in agriculture but this was supposed to happen months ago."

"Agriculture."

"The term's become meaningless, now more than ever. But this is what delay, endless delay has reduced the Institute to. Our people have to start leaving in an orderly fashion." She dug about in one of the stomachs of the file cabinet. "Here's her manifesto, quite lengthy I'm afraid." She handed Khristen a sheaf of papers covered in thin meandering lines. It resembled the excreta of some insect.

"I don't know if I can decipher this," Khristen said.

"It makes little difference. It was never particularly inspirational but she's been stalling so long it's just become a garrulous and utterly useless call to fight a battle which long ago was lost. I'll attempt to summarize."

The words *aridity, desertification, infestation, eradication, degradation, salinization* and *urbanization* occurred frequently. *Decreased resilience of the earth and her waters, vanishing resilience of the earth and her waters, vanished resilience of the earth and her waters*—the text did possess a certain acceleration though. *Biodiversity collapse* was a phrase whose horror did not accrete with repetition. An attempt was made in the closing pages to achieve a compelling narrative with an avenger in a stylish red suit becoming prominent.

"What is this red suit?"

"Oh that preposterous suit!" Lola said. "Don't bother visiting with her now. I'll call a meeting for tonight, an emergency meeting of reassessment. You'll meet everyone at last. Sundown sharp. We used to gather at the boathouse but it's too depressing there. We meet in Laundery."

LAUNDERY had been inked in scrupulous error above the rotting lintel. There were no machines in Laundery or even tubs and faucets, just broken pipes and filthy drains. The members of Lola's shabby colony sat on tables where others once had folded clean clothes. You could never have sat on one of those tables then. It

was forbidden. Several sofas that appeared to be leather and dyed a carefree pink slumped against one wall but no one had chosen to occupy them.

A man in a dirty chorister robe touched Khristen's elbow. "Rhinoceros," he said quietly, gesturing toward the sofas, "mother and childs. We try to respect them."

A small bent figure in a shrunken red suit glared at Khristen. She was leaning against a large soft woman who looked like an enormous doll.

"How old are you?" the doll asked Khristen in a pleasant fashion. When she replied, the little person beside her muttered, "She's deluded."

"Don't be mean, Scarlett," the doll said.

There was an odd little dais in one of Laundery's fetid corners and it was upon this that Lola stood beside a skeletal man with a raw and ravaged face.

"Gordon is back with us," Lola said happily, her hand on the man's arm. "I never dared hope this would happen. No applause please."

"What happened to you, Gordon?" the chorister asked. "You look dreadful. Your skin. Your whole head even."

"Later," Gordon commanded.

Lola called out names for attendance purposes. This sometimes elicited muttered assent and sometimes not. "Foxy, Hector, Grayson, Scarlett, Honey, Tom . . . Are there others?"

"It's kind of like church a little," Honey, the enormous woman, whispered to Khristen.

Lola announced James's demise. There was some difficulty among the group in remembering him. They were more reminiscent about his last subject of interest.

"I saw Frick at a Chamber of Commerce meeting once," someone said. "Merry old bastard. Life of the party."

Lola then introduced Khristen.

"Is she a guest?" a voice inquired.

"A visitor."

"I didn't think we accepted guests."

"No one's a guest here was my understanding. No visitors. No observers."

"Do you have a diagnosis at least?"

Gordon cut in impatiently. "We all have a duty here. What will you be doing to further our agenda, Khristen? Maybe you should kill all the poets. Is that something you'd be good to do?"

Khristen said nothing. It would be preposterous to express alarm of course.

"Now don't tease," Lola said.

"I'm not teasing. Killing all the poets has been a consideration for some time. They're so repulsively, tremulously anthropocentric."

"It's a fine idea," Honey said. "It's like . . . imaginative. It would require a person of considerable integrity to kill a poet."

"All the poets," Gordon corrected.

"But they don't congregate as a rule," someone said.

"Of course they congregate. There are workshops, fairs . . . slams . . ." he said distastefully.

"But what about the ones who hate and despise the world we've made," a deeply wrinkled person of girlish deportment said. "The ones who detest our ruined surroundings and the hopes and desires of those people with whom they are forced to exist? Who write unsentimentally with cold disgust . . ."

"Who are you again?" Gordon demanded.

"Foxy," Foxy said.

"You're so nineteenth century," Gordon said. "In no other age was there so much pious revulsion with the times. But even then, artists were useless. They accomplished nothing."

"Angry poets are OK, though, aren't they?" Foxy said worriedly.

Gordon sighed and his ravaged skin whistled unbecomingly. An insect bumbled against his bare arm and was snared by putrid corrugations. His exposed skin was like a Venus flytrap. He took a yellowed rag from his pocket and daubed at it. The struggling bug sunk deeper.

"You are our drug addict, is that right?" Gordon asked, seemingly having lost interest in the fate of poets. He had an unsettling voice, high-pitched and childish, quite compelling. The voices of oracles were said to be always those of children, possibly because a child can see everything in nothing whereas an adult has just the opposite inclination.

"I am," Foxy said, "I was the Queen of Rehabs. The younger generation is always trying to better me, but I consider my position unassailable. My favorite place was in North Dakota. Where they fucked over all the Indians? Or was that Oklahoma? I was there, too, I think. Anyway, they give you a hundred and fifty herbs ground up in this big disgusting shake and then you take a sauna after which you lie down in the snow and then you kneel at this communal trough with all the other junkies and puke your guts out. The next day same thing. Two weeks of this. I've probably told you about this before because, as process, it was my favorite."

The congregation was mute.

"You might be thinking I should target the pharmaceutical companies," she went on, "but I've understandably got a soft spot in my heart for them. Or I could target junkies, because they're so annoying. Why do they get to bliss out in these the most dreadful of times? But I've decided on the United States Navy instead. The annihilation of the United States Navy."

"Very good," Gordon said. "The navy has perfected their new sonar system so it always runs at maximum capability. It causes the cortex of whales and dolphins to slough off into something like cooked spaghetti. Reluctantly they have agreed to limit its peacetime use."

"Peacetime? What do they mean?" the chorister asked.

"They insist that it's essential to track submarines and is now an integral and permanent part of our defense arsenal."

"Submarines? Is anybody still making submarines?"

"I saw a whale once long ago," Honey the great doll-like woman said. "It was during a sleet storm and my girlfriend had just beaten me up again. For the last time, I told her—this is the last time you beat up on Honey and her heart of gold—and I meant it and I was sitting in my car drinking a little wine and listening to the radio and the radio was talking about a whale that had washed up on the beach that morning near the boardwalk, by the carousels, and I said to myself, 'I'm going to see that whale,' so I drove there. It was after midnight and no one was around because it wasn't sleeting anymore but it was cold and I found the whale. She was beautifully curved and glistening on the sand, like pewter, like the pewter plates my grandma used to collect. It was dark but the darkness made her body bright. Parties unknown had carved their initials deep into her sides. I stood there for the longest time in the dark. And I just wanted to kill those parties unknown. I wanted to kill them."

"Your ambitions are all admirably boundless," Gordon said. "I'm curious as to how Foxy intends to destroy the United States Navy."

"Mess with their computers. It's so easy. Like picking pockets. I have a gift."

"Must be an idiot savant," a man in sunglasses said.

Foxy shrugged. "Maybe."

Gordon scanned the room impatiently.

"You, Scarlett," he piped, "why are you still here? It's time to leave, face reality."

"I'm not at my strongest," Scarlett said.

"You're terminal," Gordon squeaked. "You don't get any stronger."

"You've got to feel the time is ripe and I have something of a headache."

"That light show at the corner of your eyes is not a celebration in your honor, it's the tumor moving in," Gordon said. "Shall I escort you out of here myself?"

"You certainly will not," Scarlett said indignantly. "You shouldn't even be back. It's highly unusual. You don't have the authority to come back."

"I'll go with you," Foxy said.

"That would be nice," Scarlett said with little enthusiasm. "My son would but his career keeps him busy. He sells his sperm. He's giving away my grandchildren right and left. He calls his jism 'White Eagle.'"

"We're glad you're back, Gordon, and I guess we're all interested in how you managed it," the man in the dark glasses said, "but you can see the problem here. Poor lady's lost it. Which brings up a number of moral concerns that weren't in play before. She can no longer be considered responsible, hell, she can no longer—"

Scarlett hissed dismissively. She had never seen old Tom without his black glasses but she imagined his eyes as two dark caves where the little bats lived. She didn't want to look at him. It was preferable to look at the aged lint congealed in a corner of Laundery, though it moved if you looked at it too long. She felt weirdly confident, amazed by the fact of her continuing existence even here. And shouldn't it be enough to feel that astonishment and have other people be happy for you? Though it seemed, actually, as her mind cleared a little, as the gaily darting lights that Gordon had so annoyingly perceived withdrew, that this amazement boded badly even, that this euphoria—this euphoric occasional confidence in being—was hardly more than a physical phenomenon prefiguring demise or dementia—whichever, really there was

hardly a hairbreadth's of difference between them—a phenomenon sometimes not so gently derided by medical professionals.

Old Tom was jawing away, now referring with little delicacy to marbles and their loss and arguing that Scarlett could no longer be sent forth to perform indifferent justice.

"Impartial," Scarlett corrected him. "Impartial justice."

Gordon grinned. His small teeth looked as though they were about to fall out of his mouth.

"I know," Scarlett assured them all. "If no one asks me I know. If I want to explain it to a questioner, I do not know."

"The problem with elderly terminals is they get canny," Tom pushed on. "They slip the bonds of conviction real quick. One minute they're with the theorem, the next they're as indisposed to dying as any civilian. And once they go gaga, they can't be utilized, it isn't ethical."

"Ethics is going to be the ruin of this operation," Gordon said. "Still, I think it would be helpful to summarize who and what as a group we are." He closed his eyes as though in prayer. They were lashless. "We are not an assisted-living facility. We are not an assisted-dying facility."

"We are not depressed, we are not suicidal. We are emotionally sober," Foxy said fiercely.

Slowly, the eyes opened. "You must have loved your little Twelve Step before you came here," Gordon said.

"So what, why not," Foxy sulked. She wondered if his pecker was as shredded and gribbled and nicked as the rest of him or whether it hung wondrously, impossibly smooth and aloof, its head like burled oak. She'd like to coax it out and mock it. Still, Gordon was kind of cool.

"Tonight is the first night of the rest of your life," Gordon warbled.

"Don't ask me to explain that first day thing," Foxy said. "I'm

not defending nobody but I learned a lot from those people. Like I felt I was made for loneliness but deep down I thought it wasn't so and then I discovered I *was* made for loneliness. Getting off the big H made me more common, sure, but I'm dedicated, I'm legit. I don't want to collapse in some line, waiting to buy a movie ticket, pissing my panties. I don't want to be in some hospital bed, gaping at some cute intern, being totally undignified in front of some cute intern. Accomplishing my death rattle for his edification. I don't want to be on the toilet. So many times people telling you about the deceased try to be discreet about it but you know the truth . . . So-and-so died parked on the toilet, making every effort . . . I want to go out like a bride, not like some bug. I want to be part of the future. Lola's given us a great opportunity here. This campaign is awesome. It's a very awesome campaign. We will bring about the collapse of the collapse recovery. We are the agents of collapse in this delicious campaign against the morally colorless and corrupt. I'm ready for a proud and wolfish death. With my death, an active death, I'll make the world more wolfish."

She stopped and looked around shyly.

Khristen heard someone whispering to her, *Why don't you speak, don't you know how to speak with us . . .*

"If I may, I want to say I'm ready now," Scarlett said. "I don't remember things like I used to but that's a gift that's given to us aged that is not sufficiently admired. Everything remembered is what's dead and everything you can't remember lives. That's what I got out of that lovely, lovely speech."

"Do you want me to go with you?" Foxy asked.

"Didn't I say that would be nice," Scarlett said. "That would be nice."

"Go then," Gordon said grandly. "Disappear into the dark, into the wet unwild, leave the butts and bounds of our poor little community, skirt the slack waters of our trapped rotting lake, this lake which reeks in silent torment, forever corrupted yet harboring

life, her green warm fish, her liquidities ever throwing themselves forward, chewing through their obscure element, ever toward no new place, no promised country or other shore . . ."

"Ah Gordon, you have a way with the words," the chorister said.

"The womb of nature and perhaps her grave," said Lola.

An enormous cockroach sauntered across the floor. Honey startled as a memory stirred within her remarkable chest, the irreducible essence of her high school days returning to her with its odor of lipstick and wool. There was a chemistry teacher they were all mad for. He once demonstrated how a cockroach without its head could learn not to dip its leg in water from which it received a shock.

"I think our problem—one of our problems anyway—is acclimatization," Tom said. "Who could imagine that it was possible to become accustomed to these rooms, this lake, these . . ." he indicated the group with a vague sweep of his hand, ". . . companions. When I first came here I had visions. They'd come in waves. Boom Boom Boom. It's been days, weeks now since I've had one."

Honey watched the cockroach which was the size of a kitten vanish under a splintered baseboard. Oh, she'd thought the world of that chemistry teacher. He'd certainly been the handsomest man in town.

"Acclimatization is very much a concern," Gordon said. He smiled and his teeth looked like small golden fish resting in the darkness of his mouth.

I miss . . . Khristen thought, I miss . . . She felt transfixed, impaled, untranslated. She'd changed so much so as not to miss it even more, for that's how you change—by missing something too much and pretending not to.

"What happened to ya, Gordon," the chorister called out. "You look very awful. Scaly, speckled. A dead ringer for a ghost."

"I had gone forth," Gordon said. "I harbored no hope of returning to you."

The chorister nodded, stroking the sofa fretfully.

"The weather, as would be expected, was extreme. The wind! The wind here is but a breeze compared to it. I found myself on a wide road leading to my destination. The wires of great fallen poles struck out at me and lashed me as I walked and I accepted their bitings and lashings."

"You got a number of infections I think," Hector noted.

"It was later revealed to me that the wires had been favored by certain assemblies of birds at their toilette. Larks."

"Larks!"

"Once known for their jubilant song and their pathetic habit of nesting on the ground."

"How ironic that it would be the humble lark," Hector said.

"Flesh-eating microbes have now taken up residence on my body," Gordon said. "I am told that I'm not infectious, not that that would trouble you, I assume. I admit that I rather enjoyed returning, walking through the great repulsed or pitying throngs of this tumbreled world. Repulsed or pitying, the emotions have become so similar. Some were angered that they were forced to perceive me, my appearance, but most ignored me, denied me. Denial is now an art, a social grace, a survival tool, as is apathy which has become a sign of refinement." He paused, and with a peculiar gesture crossed his arms over his chest. "What was your experience?"

After a moment, Khristen realized he was addressing her. "I didn't return, I just arrived," she said.

"That's true, Gordon," Lola said.

Some reiterated the understanding that guests were not permitted among their number. This was no place for observers or visitors. The motel was provided for the rather distasteful concept

of guests. The motel, where figures lounged about talking about nothing in particular as though nothing had happened.

"Maybe you can tell us a little more of the situation out there, Gordon," Tom said. "What's the moral temperature of the population?"

"I just love the way he talks sometimes," Honey confided to Khristen.

"People who lack all sympathy are feeling better about themselves. The more a person doesn't care the freer he becomes. The new thinking is that compassion is nothing but self-cannibalization." Gordon yawned, a fearsome sight.

"Any centralized command?" Tom asked. "Guidance from any quarter?"

"Any art?" the chorister wondered. "I suppose worship has fallen off?"

"There's the usual useless guidance. Worship is negligible. Art's decor, and is mostly confined to depictions of the harrow. Some of it's pretty abstract but if people can be assured it's a harrow it will find acceptance. Representations of the harrow are in all government facilities that remain and homes are encouraged to display the image as well. It started out as a bit of nostalgia but devolved into a sign of respect, of self-acknowledgment. No one gives thanks to it of course, just respect. It's a unifying symbol. Says, *We will not be overcome*. Pretty much everything is up and running again. The amusement industry has heroically reestablished itself. Disney World has rebooted and is going strong."

*"Disney World!"* The chorister paled. He had suffered his first extreme breakdown there when he perceived his archenemy, the magnificent and unapproachable thurifer, approaching him in deceitful welcome costumed as Minnie Mouse.

"The mega-technological fantasy of glorified and constant consumption in controlled and utopian worlds which prepare

people psychologically for life in denatured artificial environments has never been more popular."

"Does it rain there still?" Hector said. "Is it spring? It must be about time."

"Outside of entertainment there's more subservience, more allegiance to a non-conciliatory unified and robust response to threat. All that is non-human is considered detrimental to the future. All conservation attempts are considered reactionary. Any suggestion to repair or renew our relationship with nature is perceived as an attempt to exploit a crisis. People think the planet is attempting to make threats—the withdrawal of spring—and nonnegotiable demands, and it pisses them off."

*. . . I've thought about you and thought about you,* Khristen heard the voice say faintly, *and wondered when I'd see you again . . .*

"There are few prohibitions," Gordon went on, waving away the moths that were approaching him in wonder. "Rules are considered too onerous in this time of stress. People have to blow off steam. Arson has become popular again. Let this fucking land of ours that has turned against us burn, is the prevailing sentiment." Gordon regarded his purulent knuckles, worse on the left than the right.

"What about our exhortations that were always part of our actions?" Honey asked. "Weren't they occasionally persuasive? Scarlett wrote a highly detailed informative paper, didn't she? I never read it but . . ."

"No need to bother with manifestos anymore. There's no interest in tolerating arguments for paradigm shifts."

"So those who've gone before us . . . their efforts haven't made any difference then?" Honey said.

"Just added to the general mayhem. Of course no one's put two and two together yet concerning the resort here and more directed sabotage out there."

"Are suicides prevalent?" Tom asked.

"Figures are way down. The few that occur are committed in the old-fashioned manner, onanistically, without addressing social, ecological or spiritual issues."

"You've certainly brought back sobering news," Tom said. "Grave news, I mean."

"That unfortunately is my report," Gordon said. "Or most of it anyway."

"So much to absorb," Lola said. "I regret we can't adjourn on a more positive note. But keep in mind, everyone, that nothing must affect our obligations, and prompt departure times must still be met."

*Poor old carling*, someone sighed, and Khristen realized she had heard more voices than there were beings in this looted yet still accommodating room because there really weren't many of them there.

It was time for reflection, Honey reflected. She would maneuver around Gordon's assessment somehow, keep her spirits high. Their deaths *would* matter. They *would* effect, what did he call it, a paradigm shift, the earth *would* heal as a result of their actions, balance and beauty *would* return.

She decided she'd stay in the courtyard tonight, her legs were too tired to carry her to her room. She liked the courtyard, where fragments from the resort's carefree past could still work their way up through the dirt to the surface—cribbage pegs, lanyards, confetti. You really couldn't call it dirt anymore, least of all soil, because some worm had come through and changed its composition but the stuff was generally referred to as dirt, it being accepted that it was too much trouble to define it as something else.

She settled herself down cautiously. Heart of gold and limbs of lead and several minds directing the whole apparatus. She tried to suppress her longing to have her Cadillac back. Like a great

beamy boat it had been transporting the cargo of her body. It would take her anywhere she chose to go. It was harder to get around now, even here, particularly here.

She was old now and it had taken her far too many years to arrive but she could still pinpoint the moment when a chain of events culminated in a debt it had taken her decades to pay off. But that was what happened in a world where you were asleep and made sleepy accommodations as a dreamer would, in a dream.

The first links of the chain appeared in the semblance of a man wanting to resurface her driveway. A few hours later it was a man who wanted to repair the crack in the Caddy's windshield. She couldn't even see it but he detected it and offered to fix it. Someone wanted to prune her trees, hang up holiday lights. Life is too short to clean your own house, a woman told her vehemently. Lastly arrived the vendor with the fish. She was outside, then, still in her bathrobe, wondering what was killing the birds again. She had stopped feeding them, hoping the problem would resolve itself but it had not. A stumpy truck clattered up her driveway.

"Look," she said, "I don't even own this place. I'm renting."

"I want to sell you some beautiful fresh fish. For supper. Join my club for a small fee and each week I'll deliver a beautiful fish to your drawer."

"Drawer!" she exclaimed, laughing.

"Door, door, of course," he said irritably. He had orange hair and wore mirrored glasses.

"No, no, no. No fish. I sympathize with you having to drive around like this trying to make a few bucks but no. No fish."

He darted around to the back of the truck and raised the door. "Look. Just look please, then decide."

Something of the purest white with a long needle-like snout lay on a shelf from which water hung in gelid strings.

"What is that?" Honey asked.

"Its head doesn't have eyes in it. See? The real thing."

"The real thing," Honey said. "What is it?"

"From China, this fish. *Baiji*. From the Yangtze."

"But how did it get here?"

"Truck. Refrigeration. Latest large aquatic mammal driven to extinguishment. Before that, it was, oh gee, the Caribbean monk seal in the fifties."

Honey, in her favorite bathrobe, had never felt more vulnerable and decided on the spot that she would discontinue this swanning around in the old comfy thing of a morning.

"I wouldn't know how to prepare it," she said. "I'm not much of a cook."

"Just like with anything. A little oil. Shallots if you've got."

She saw her bathrobe in his glasses, a wildly cubed and patterned thing. It was as if she were a fly looking at herself.

"What if I offered this whole fish to you for two dollars."

"Why don't I give you two dollars and a Coke and you keep it," Honey said quickly.

He ran his hands through his orange hair, considering.

"You know," Honey said, "I'm a blood donor. I have an appointment this morning actually to give blood. I should have left already."

"OK," he said. "Two Cokes and two bucks."

In the house she quickly changed into a long skirt, boots and several sweaters. She was very cold. She took two Cokes out of the refrigerator and a ten-dollar bill out of her purse, and hurried back outside.

He was sitting in the cab, looking impatient.

"Here," she said, "thank you very much."

He took the offerings and looked at her disdainfully. Water shot from the truck's bed as he accelerated away.

She was driving to the Bloodmobile in her big gray Cadillac, wondering if she'd locked the house. She'd like to move away now more than ever. Sweet Jesus that fish! but as people always

said, *Where you gonna go? Every place is like every place else* . . .
What was she doing even renting a house anyway? She was a free
spirit. When she'd seen that whale on the beach all carved up by
drunks and pranksters she thought her life would become differ-
ent but she'd just become more earthbound and maybe even more
susceptible to horrid situations.

She sat mulling at a red light at a gigantic intersection. The
light turned green and she floored it, she was so late, it was past
actually the . . . An object smashed into the passenger door of the
Cadillac, T-boning the door to a modest degree. The object, a
sports car with the vanity plate MUVORER, became airborne, flying
like a crumpled Kleenex into a cement utility pole by which it was
trephined with glittering efficiency.

Honey was taken to the hospital for observation, though her
only apparent injury was a bitten lip. Someone stole her purse
as she was assisted into the ambulance but she had scissored her
credit cards long before. Honey had never been able to handle the
responsibilities of credit. That purse wasn't going to get anyone
anywhere.

The sports car's driver—blatantly dead—had been the re-
nowned commercial real estate developer Eddie Emerald, driving
to close on a refugium of international significance. The elitists
and extremists and anti-humanists who thought they'd secured
the refugia aspects of the refugiums long ago at considerable cost
and compromise found they hadn't at all. There was a comma in
a place where it wasn't supposed to be. Or it was a comma absent
from a place where it was supposed to be. The plans were still
fluid as to how the properties would be utilized, but a Supercuts
had shown interest in a slice of the site which comprised some
stunning acreage.

The environmental community was ecstatic at the news of
Eddie's death. Eddie Emerald gone! Eddie Fucking Emerald offed
by a fatty in a Caddy. Honey became as a goddess to them.

At the hospital the decision was made to keep her for observation—a week or two at the most, they said. Something was amiss with her but the doctors couldn't determine what. She *was* large, but she didn't at all look her age, which she reluctantly disclosed. She had always had good skin and being practically gigantic, everyone knew, kept you looking younger longer. You'd ask anybody to guess her age and they'd be off at the very least by ten years unless they sensed a trick and threw out a figure that wasn't sincere.

It was when she was in the hospital that she discovered the cell in the basement, not a cell naturally with bars and a cold floor but a group of people who considered themselves a Cell. There were never more than half a dozen of them. They sat around a scarred table under bright fluorescent lights and listened to a pleasant voice emitting from a tape recorder. They didn't believe in reality the way most people believed in it, was the nearest Honey could get to what they believed in. Though "belief" wasn't even the proper word. When the recording was over, the leader—she guessed he was the leader even if he seemed self-effacing to a fault—made a few comments in a soft voice. Sometimes someone would ask a question, making a stab at clarification, she supposed. *Is this the same as this?* Or, *Don't you think we ought to . . .* The answer was always no. There was never any wine or cookies or juice. The hour was not at all companionable. Still, the meetings thrilled her in some anxious way though there was very little she could retain from the discussions. Once there was some talk about the Net. The Net holds the person who is asleep by ropes and cords and pulleys and hooks. The Net holds us fast. The Net exists even in the Underworld and the dead regard it with dismay and abhorrence. The subject of the Net was then dropped. Someone quietly remarked that a person who is not horrified by himself knows nothing of himself.

Then the Cell moved elsewhere. The room was taken over

evenings by an investment seminar. No one knew where the Cell had gone or under what banner they had managed to obtain the room in the first place as it was primarily reserved for CPR instruction or lactation classes.

Honey was bereft. It was around this time that the environmental groups stopped sending flowers and grateful notes to her room because Eddie Emerald's widow had gone ahead with the dozing and flattening of the refugium even though her legal right to do so was in doubt. The blading of the site was done the morning the scrappy developer was buried, as a final tribute to him. At the same time the mourners were enjoying post-internment cocktails and munchies at the DoubleTree, the announcement was made to whooping applause that the land was 100-percent leased out, In-N-Out-Burger, an organic farmer's market and a car and truck detailing station were the last lucky tenants. Eddie Emerald might be gone but so was the pocket wilderness. Honey might even have accelerated its death, some activists groused. Fucking Eddie had been the devil they knew and occasionally he had tossed them a bone. And now he was no more.

The hospital was abruptly eager to discharge her. Whatever Honey had was unusual and fatal but the doctors with their poking and prodding and questioning had gotten pretty much all they could out of her without cutting her open, a suggestion she rejected, she hoped, with grace and good nature. She was susceptible to her lost basement's Cell's idea that self-annihilation was necessary for spiritual rebirth but she didn't think that consigning herself into the curious hands of surgeons at this undistinguished institution was what they meant.

The nurses said goodbye, gave her the usual—the plastic pan, the bath wipes, the Sure-Grip socks, the tube of moisturizing lotion, the complimentary magazine.

"It might take you a little longer than you'd think to read these

articles," a nurse suggested. "Your comprehension might be down a bit."

While she was waiting for a wheelchair to remove her she read about a seven-year-old who got fourteen years in the slammer for environmental activism. If she'd had even one milk tooth left in her head she wouldn't have fallen under the terrorism enhancement sentencing guidelines but she didn't so she had. The child's name wasn't being released because of her age but the journalist did provide the detail that she was no higher than a tabletop which meant that she couldn't even attend a carnival ride unattended. But what had the poor kid done anyway? Honey couldn't seem to extract this information from the article. "Punishing crimes in the name of the environment is our highest priority," the successful prosecutor was quoted as saying.

The phrasing seemed wily in the extreme, but Honey feared the nurse might have a point. Her comprehension had begun to fray.

A bill was presented and at last a wheelchair was provided. In it she was pushed to the curb. She owed the place over three hundred thousand dollars which she naturally lacked the means to pay. They assured her they would hound her to the ends of the earth and beyond if necessary to collect these funds.

She had lingered outside the hospital's doors for some time. It was eerily silent and the air smelled sharp and acrid. Nothing was particularly recognizable to her, nothing seemed suited to her nature. She walked a few yards and it became dark quickly. Then it was day again and she was cooling her swollen feet in the tepid waters of a sorry-looking lake. Yellow scum tickled her ankles. It felt nice though, no doubt about that. Her poor feet blessed her for her presence of mind in an untenable situation. The people here weren't as intriguing as those in the Cell but they weren't all that different from them either. They didn't seem to be in full pos-

session of their faculties but who was these days? She sometimes entertained the thought she'd died in her dear old Caddy and that this was death. But if that were the situation then everyone here would have to be dead as well which was possible if unlikely, even that new girl who'd shown up who seemed so familiar but who was not. And if that were the situation why were there so few of them and why were the demands being made upon them so futile given their condition? The world seemed to be proceeding as it always had, it hadn't ended after all, which was strange too.

She'd been so discouraged once, *so* discouraged, and even this place could make her blue. For example, the story about the whale, the story that meant so much to her, had scarcely been acknowledged, and she was sure she hadn't mentioned it before, which would have been tiresome she guessed.

She tried to settle down and enjoy the night which enveloped her not that comfortably, though she preferred it to the days, which mostly had a rubbery, unforgiving texture. This place was outside the perimeter of death, she assured herself. Or was it *parameter* she wondered . . .

The next morning it was determined that Foxy had gone but Scarlett was still in residence.

"Please go and coax her out," Lola begged Khristen. "Tell her Gordon has arranged for a car and driver."

Scarlett was not at all pleased to see Khristen.

"Do you want me to call an ambulance?" Khristen asked.

"The ambulance doesn't come out here, girl, don't you know a thing! What's the matter with you! Who are you anyway!"

She was complaining about this pain, this new pain, way down . . . "It's like I want to take a dump but I can't. Is that kidney stones? Gallbladder?"

"Your suit's all ready to go. Why, you're even wearing it!" Khristen exclaimed. "And I've just been informed that Gordon has arranged for a car and driver."

"I bet he has," Scarlett said crossly. "Those two love to arrange for a car and driver."

She'd been given eight months to live and was coming up on the end of it. Initially she'd been quite excited about her role in this lunatic venture.

"Your mission might make a difference," Khristen said. "Insecticides, pesticides, herbicides, there are no restrictions on their use whatever. This might make people question . . ."

"You can't stop the bastards. I'd just be offing an underling or two. It wouldn't affect the corporate level at all. I must say though that meeting last night was almost enough to push me out the door."

"What happened to Foxy?"

"Who knows. She's a bit weird, don't you think? All she wants to do is repent which quite narrows her potential."

"She seemed pretty determined."

"Oh she's not as smart as she thinks she is. But the rest of them—they have no more sense than a Pluto Platter."

"What's that?"

"A Pluto Platter?"

"Yes."

"Well it started out as a pot lid I believe. For a popcorn pot. But the concept became plastic. You sail it through the air. But it doesn't return to you, that's something else." She looked at Khristen and emitted a burp.

"Did you have a favorite part of being here?" Khristen asked. "You've been here for a while now."

"I guess my favorite part was thinking of the people who knew me back when, if they were still around, saying 'Why, we didn't

know her at all! Who knew she was capable of murder. And on behalf of the earth at that!' " Scarlett gently kneaded her stomach, "That gave me a good feeling, thinking that."

"Well they can say those things for real now. Lola said you had a lot of scatter pins. Do you want to be wearing all your scatter pins?"

"For real!" Scarlett mocked. There were scatter pins, she supposed, but she preferred to think of them as medals. She would be a general, terribly attractive, marching into battle with all that sauce or salad or whatever they called it on her chest . . . But that came later. You didn't wear them during the actual battle. That would be in poor taste. "I'm not going to do it," she announced. "I want to be remembered as a respectable person. I don't want to do anything wrong."

"Do you ever think we're here because we did something wrong already?"

"You are so exasperating. I want to tell you something. I believe I'm hungry! I haven't had an appetite for ever so long and now I want a cucumber sandwich. Would you be so kind as to get me one?"

"What about the statement you wrote?"

"Give it to the next one."

"But it's yours. You put a lot of thought into it."

"Who's next in the pipeline? They can use it. I think that maybe one of the problems was that the filet knife is just too intimate and I've seen these young men in photographs and they're unexceptional in every way. Selling poison is their job. I'm sure they don't think it's anything to get stuck in the ribs for."

A bit of color had crept into Scarlett's old cheeks.

"You look as though you signed a new lease on life," Khristen said.

"I don't believe you sign it, you get . . ."

"There is no lease, it's imaginary," Khristen said.

Scarlett gazed at her coldly.

"Lola says personal existence vanishes unless it is stabilized and consolidated in radical and sustained acts of choice," Khristen said.

"I know she says that! Don't I know she drums that into us! But like most of what Lola says, it doesn't stand up to scrutiny. Personal existence departs a person regardless. Lola's just trying to stir things up, you know. Before this notion she had the Hemlock Society out here but that wasn't lively enough for her, oh no. She had the same problem with them. When it came time, people backed off. You could wheedle them ragged, it wouldn't convince them, not usually. Lola took the Hemlock idea, a Mr. Derek Humphry's idea by way of Socrates, and gave it a twist is all, a very naughty twist. She's practically a plagiarist . . ." She looked at Khristen suspiciously. "Did you know my Fred?"

Khirsten shook her head.

"I had so many dreams last night and he was in every one of them. I was outside this fine old house Fred and I had lived in, looking at it, a wonderful house, beautiful wood throughout, those darling thumb-latch doors, the kind of ceilings those atheist architects call cathedral, four fireplaces, a slate roof, gardens and orchards, a gazebo . . ."

Surely the woman was exaggerating, Khristen thought.

". . . and there was Fred, hustling toward it while I watched and I called out to him, 'We don't live there anymore, it's not even there, it's a Walgreens,' and he said, 'That doesn't matter to me now.' They tore that beautiful old house down and it wasn't even on a corner. Walgreens made it all a corner. Hundreds of people materialize in the aisles hourly, tramping around, buying cheap cheese and batteries, sticking their arms in those blood pressure sleeves. Don't you tell me there's any sacredness to places."

"I won't," Khristen said.

"All last night it was Fred, Fred, Fred. I recall a week to the day before he went, he said, 'I want a copy of *Boating World Magazine*,'

and so I went to the newsstand and got him a copy of *Boating World Magazine*. Then the day before he went, he said, 'I want a year's subscription to *Boating World Magazine*,' and everyone could tell he wouldn't be seeing next Tuesday and I said, 'Fred, don't you be childish. You know that's twelve issues, arriving singly over the course of a year, a whole year,' I said. I feel bad about that, my reaction. It wouldn't have killed me to have gotten the poor man a subscription, picked up the phone, made a big show out of getting him a good faith subscription."

"You should feel bad about that," Khristen said.

"Are you going to get that cucumber sandwich or not," Scarlett demanded. "Very little mayonnaise." She dismissed the exasperating presence from her mind and smoothed the sleeves of her suit. The skin of her hands was like crepe. What had she been meant for? Surely she was not meant to become the agent in the murders of some pesticide representatives. She was no anarchist and what was demeaning about that? She wasn't a transgressor. Break what must be broken. Yes. Perhaps. But she was not a breaker. Besides, there were hundreds of young fellows working for pesticide companies and worse with families to support. Why didn't Lola aim for the people at the top, the ones least indirectly responsible? Because she abhorred research was why. She didn't want to do the research required to find the individual solely accountable. Her organization could use an overhaul. It was nothing but a grubby little suicide academy.

She pictured one of the fools whose life she had spared. He wore a wedding ring. He would be going home tonight to some ghastly little family—*them*—instead of lying in a public atrium by a smelly water fountain not responding to resuscitation efforts. The more she thought about him the more resentful she became. She didn't want to be responsible for having preserved another's future. If she were that sort of person she would have stuck with the little girl from the Dominican Republic she and Fred had

adopted, Natalie Ann. She lived with them for nine years and she was all right, not exactly what you'd call a joy to be around but a good little girl by and large, no trouble at all really; then she hit puberty and began to masculinize, started turning into a boy that can't be a boy without a great deal of financial investment. Scarlett found this disconcerting. You couldn't even come out of a movie theater with her without someone yelling across the parking lot *Hey blackhead are you a boy or a girl:* Scarlett just didn't feel up to the challenge. She and Fred went back to the agency and were told that this was unexceptional, in fact it was exceptionally common, it had something to do with the Dominican Republic. *Didn't nobody tell you?* they said. *It's against the rules not to tell* . . . Fred didn't want to give the child up but Scarlett had said *Natalie Ann will be the death of me!!* Fred hadn't much spine to him but he wasn't lazy either. If you could get him going, he'd accomplish what was necessary. He determined that men from the Dominican Republic usually get themselves employed as duct cleaners and the like and Fred contacted a duct cleaning business and set up an appointment. The workers agreed to take the child for inclusion in their families in exchange for a Chevy Silverado with a tow package and no more than forty thousand miles on the engine. Following the removal of Natalie Ann they had one of their own—so strange because they thought they couldn't—a boy, the one who made a living selling sperm, of all things. The years hurtled by. Fred was an actuary, she believed that's what he'd been, and she taught second graders for a while, though only as a sub, always a sub. There was a game they played. *Once I was a . . . and now I am a . . .* How they loved that game, the little ones. *Once I was a crayon but now I am six o'clock at night.*

She couldn't remember who she'd been anymore.

Fred had wanted UNTIL WE MEET AGAIN on his tombstone.

She had said, *Fred, will you never stop torturing me. You're going to be the death of me, Fred.*

At the end when you're old and bedridden you should just want to be quiet but Fred hadn't been quiet. They'd had to give him morphine, he was so upset. They call you once they give them the morphine.

She would have to turn the light on soon if she were to see anything. Another day gone. What was it she was waiting for?

The sandwich.

That girl would never bring it. That girl had forgotten all about it and her, too, just because she hadn't shivved a fellow indirectly responsible for the deaths of thousands of butterflies. Or was it millions? Lola needed an accountant. She was so vague with figures. And had it even been butterflies at all, or those other things? Chry . . . chry . . . the cocoon things. The ones that slept and turned into, slept and turned into . . . something else.

She was wanting something still, even if she couldn't remember it. They'd better not count her out yet.

She began to fuss with the light. The day had become a little dim. The lamp was supposed to have three degrees of brightness—it had one of those fancy bulbs. But you can't put one of those fancy bulbs into an inferior socket, well not inferior exactly but one that's just not set up right . . .

In the distance something leapt about in the sky like lightning. Khristen was making her circuit around the lake. *Pronounced.* The word appeared in her mind as though upon the path. Like a great wilted flower. *Pronounced.* It was a word they used before the dead in that instant when everything was altered. She pushed past it, its petaled softness. Several trails branched away from the muddy path that encircled Big Girl in morose embrace. She turned onto the one that led to the motel.

Jeffrey was seated under a rotting awning wearing a suit and tie.

"You're wearing a suit and tie," she noted.

"You don't know how to speak with me yet, do you," he said.

"Are you leaving?"

"Oh you'll know when I leave." He looked past her in proud disguise.

"Will you be telling me then?"

"I have no idea when I'll be leaving!" He pointed toward his mother, prone, flawlessly bronzed in a black swimsuit, a red and white cooler by her side. "It's all up to her. And she doesn't know. She doesn't know anything. It's her drinking. But if she stopped drinking this very night she would not recognize me tomorrow."

"Who would she see instead?"

"No idea." He removed his tie. It was patterned with small oars. "King or courier, you know that game, don't you? It's a children's game. Who would you rather be?"

"The king's friend."

"You're so sincere," he said glumly. "But I don't find sincerity intolerable like many people do. I'm quite tolerant though it may not seem so, it may not appear that I'm at all tolerant but Mother has put me in some very uncomfortable situations and I've had to make the best of them."

He removed his black suit jacket, then pulled his shirt over his head. His skin was white as an infant's tooth and he appeared quite emaciated. No one seemed driven to partake of nourishment here. The snack machines gleaming in dark alcoves were empty and unplugged. He replaced the shirt over his head, though backward.

"We're passing through, just passing through. Isn't that what they say?"

"I guess some people say it."

"Though for the moment you're not passing through at all. You're over there, associating with those alarmingly misinformed people and I'm confined here to Unit One. *Grebe*. All the rooms are named after birds that lived here once, not in the motel of course. Grebes are diving birds. Unassuming little things."

"Are the rooms different inside?" She pictured carefully inscribed murals, trompe l'oeil floors, distinctive dioramas, nests of varying commitment and design.

"One would think, but I doubt it. Decor is so seldom edifying. I no longer find life to be as edifying as I once did. You could argue that it was misrepresented to me because of my youth. I had my tata and my law library. I was not afraid of the dentist, I . . ." He looked with sudden alarm at the empty swimming pool. "Where is my swan?" After a moment of study, he said, "Well, it's gone."

"The wind perhaps," Khristen suggested.

"I believe you were told I was at the dentist. Well, I was not," he said.

They were silent. She thought of chapel, back at her school's monthly Taizé service when someone would forget to tap the chime, probably deliberately, and you would wait and wait on your knees until one of the smaller kids would begin to cry.

"*Grebe,*" he said at last. "That is a gesture only."

"Yes," she said. "Someone's gesture."

"The real work will begin when we're gone from here. Even for you. Mother says you think you've already died. That's why you give her the creeps."

"Some time ago, I was told that. By my mother actually."

"They always want something more from us, don't they. They're never satisfied. They believe in progress through the generations. Super abilities and such. Increased comprehension. I will never have issue. The line will stop with me."

It was not difficult to believe this.

"Did you see runners on your way here. People running?"

"No runners," Khristen said.

"You came from a different direction. We saw so many! And giant billboards everywhere! RUN FOR BABIES. The billboards depicted a large hand and in this hand was a tiny human creature. RUN FOR BABIES mile after mile, but Mother was driving at such

a high rate of speed it was some time before I noticed that the date for the marathon was incorrect. All those people were running for something else. Mother just raced right through them. She might even have struck several."

The wind rose, searching the sky for something to engage, then finding nothing, dropped down to nudge the water in the pool.

"Do you know that doves can fly several hundred miles a day?"

"I did not," Khristen said.

"But they usually didn't. Now they don't at all."

Barbara stirred on the chaise lounge and sat upright. She gazed at them saying nothing for a moment then said, "Oh my God." She rooted around in the cooler. "Darling," she said to Jeffrey, "would you bring me one of those jars from the refrigerator, one of those quart jars? How many are left, have you noticed?"

"Five," he said.

"Oh my God! No, forget it, darling. Mustn't make you my Ganymede." She stood and entered Grebe. "God, only five."

"She's not seeing you anymore," Jeffrey noted. "She can't focus on reversals. I suppose that's for the best. She revels in distress but it's not good for her. She could have a cerebral hemorrhage or something," he said thoughtfully. "Of course I'm no doctor. But you're no housekeeper either."

"It was suggested," she said, startled. "But . . ."

"Though we could use some towels . . . Just kidding!" he crowed, jumping up and down in the most awkward fashion. "I was immersing myself in maritime law this morning and that always makes me a little silly afterward. But that awful little woman in the Santy Claus suit . . . you were supposed to bring her something, a sandwich I believe."

"Oh, I was! A cucumber sandwich. I forgot. She must be—"

"Don't concern yourself about it. The sandwich could not possibly have been provided."

"Perhaps she decided to set off after all, and she only wanted

me to leave her alone. I don't even know where the bread is kept," Khristen worried. "I could never have come back with a sandwich. I hope I didn't promise her I would."

The wind glided away from the pool, pushing at a bit of refuse as a dog might with his nose, considering its worth.

"This operation is clearly winding down, what's puzzling is that you've arrived for it," Jeffrey mused. "We could hear your voices the other night, voices carry you know. Mother thought it was a hoot. She finds the provincial hilarious."

"It was a meeting," Khristen said. "Someone who had left and was not expected back returned."

"We determined that more or less from the babble. The one who returned sounds positively frightful."

"He spoke about the condition of the world we'd known. There's been quite a lot of renewal, he said—that is, much that brought about so much destruction has been restored."

"Oh look!" Jeffrey exclaimed. "A backgammon board." He prodded at something in the ground. "But only half of it."

"The people present thought there was still time for them to sacrifice themselves for a better purpose but apparently there is not."

"Oldest game in recorded history," Jeffrey noted. He looked at Khristen. "I am very impressed by the use of the word *renewal*. Excellent employment of judicial review."

"I find words are becoming more and more treacherous," she admitted.

"Never trust them, my tata says. Bend them to your will."

She had traveled here through a riven world but she remembered even then seeing, on the distant mountains shorn of any green, the machines and cables spanning them, tiny as toys and slim as strings, and figures trembling and shifting there with tireless purpose as though the intention was to raise the dead peaks for the sole purpose of burying them again.

"Other than the runners, what did you see before you arrived?"

she asked Jeffrey. For she felt as uncertain about visions as the words that accompanied them.

"Food trucks and armament. A great deal of armament. My tata says it's because they gave a tax break to households with guns. Now no one pays taxes because everyone has guns." He gave a short bark of amusement. "No provisions have been made for consequences."

Armament and food trucks. It had been a bit of a blur coming here. Tongue tacos had been heavily advertised. The tongues of angels could possibly be provided if one knew the right contacts. Variety was in more demand than ever.

"Would you be able to tell me . . ." she began.

"I'm a child," he said reasonably. "I'm but ten." He put his jacket back on and buttoned it.

"Yes," Khristen said. "I was at your birthday party. At the bowling alley."

He was about to tease her and reply that his birthday event, which she had attended, true, was certainly not at a bowling alley—surely she must have suspected that—but she was so easily troubled he decided not to.

"Strikes and spares," he said. "Awful racket. All quite meaningless."

"I wonder if it's still there."

"Of course it isn't there, still or not! And those sentimental chimps of Lola's aren't there. We're all being fed the most awful drivel. We're consuming nothing but lies."

The frolic he always briefly felt after momentarily quitting the rigors of maritime law was fading and he felt desperate to return to his books—the ponderous certainties of text and the resisting ineffable sea.

They both stared at the pool, mindful again of the absent swan. He felt cross. It had been a wobbling luffing heap of profoundly indestructible plastic. It couldn't possibly have disappeared.

Tom paced by a cracked fish tank. It held a cheesy chipped grotto and a toppled Neptune—formerly reckoned as one of the great gods, ruler of the deep, lord of both salt water and fresh—astraddle a dented can of energy drink.

This was not what Lola commanded as her office but another lobby-like space in the once grand structure. The hotel complex had once been enormous with every amenity. There'd even been plans in its heyday to enclose the whole enchilada in a polymer bubble like the ski slopes in Dubai. It had a bunker-like feel to it now, a last station feel.

For years, Tom had worked with germs. Tularemia, Q fever, brucellosis, glanders, plague . . . but he was never a natural like his father. His father had been one of the first germ warriors, one of the best. He and his team had developed the incapacitants for an assault on Cuba. Debilitate for a few hours, incapacitate for a few weeks. The entire island would go down in a benign biological assault enabling conventionally armed troops to go in without casualties. It was beautifully nuanced. A few hundred Cubans might die, maybe a thousand, but they would have been those with prior health issues. Statistically they were irrelevant.

His father had not been bitter about the failure to implement. "They ask you to solve a problem and you do and that's when the quibbling begins. It'll always be that way," he said. "Don't let them sweet-talk you into defense. Insist on offense. Defense is more complicated and never as satisfying. It takes ten months to develop a weapons-grade agent and ten more years to develop a vaccine against it."

The project Tom devoted himself to was called *Aeolus*. His wife often teased him about the *real* Aeolus who had six sons and six daughters all living together on a precipitous isle. Caroline hoped for six and six. She was not about to let her husband's

occupation sour her on the future. But she bore no babies, it was cancer that found her to be a fruitful host. Throughout her long decline he continued with his work. He traveled to Russia for brief but frequent periods, working with researchers there. But he was becoming uneasily unprofessional. The smell of bleach and straw and animal agony, the broken vivariums, the stalls and cages, the posts with tethering rings on the dried seabeds. His colleagues assured him that the most exciting discoveries all lay ahead. The rescripting of human metabolism was in its infancy, the manipulation of immune systems had just begun. It was the purity of possibility that made his bug and gas colleagues blue-sky optimists. Germs could be designed not only to kill but to manage all of life's processes—cognition, development, reproduction, everything. If there was anyone out there who still thought they knew what it meant to be human, their world was about to change.

At some point the project's name was changed from *Aeolus* to *Renaissance*, even though Tom argued that the Russians had already grabbed that word, *Vozrozhdeniye*, for their collapsed undertaking. A new hire, considered enormously talented in her work of inducing a condition known as "horror autotoxicus" in mice, said that the word was goddamned nearly unpronounceable and that the Russians only claimed that was what it meant. And what standing did the Russians have anyway in any of their considerations? Her views carried the day.

After Caroline died, he returned to Russia where he acquired a serious vodka dependency and did watercolors—surprisingly easy to execute—of the poisoned steppes. He worked with anthrax, played volleyball when he wasn't too hung over and tried to get his nerve back.

Sometimes he'd go to the cemetery outside the old testing grounds with his Russian friends. They were always stumbling drunk, they would pour vodka on the graves of those who had accidentally infected themselves with the viruses they were weap-

onizing. "This one here," one of them shouted over the wind, "was buried with the notebook where he documented the progress of his hemorrhagic fever. Hemorrhaging like your Old Faithful. A hero. A real man." Beneath the tumbled plots lay the zinc-lined coffins. The wind shrieked and moaned. Once they'd left the door open on the sedan they'd arrived in and it was ripped off to fly across the ashen land like a cafeteria tray.

When he finally came home, his clearance was revoked and he was fired.

He loitered around the house for a few months drinking and watching the weeds recolonize his neglected yard. In his opinion, it took the utility companies a remarkably long time to turn off the electric, gas and water for nonpayment, but when they did, he put the ironwood box that contained his wife's ashes on the passenger seat of his Jaguar and drove away. After hundreds of miles he stopped at a bar and was surprised to learn it was New Year's Eve. "Amateur night," the bartender said, looking at him distrustfully. Bugs Bunny cartoons played on a screen in the corner. "He used to be a deity," the woman on the stool beside him said loudly and not to him, "and look what they've done to him, they've taken away his powers." When he emerged some hours later under the somber regard of a starless sky, he realized, though not immediately, that the Jaguar had been stolen.

He had the worst hangover of his life. It was blinding, unprecedented. But even after it had slowly passed, he sensed that his vision had been compromised and would no longer be performing its previously reliable duties. Cornea, iris, pupil, lens, retina, optic nerve. Even when the whole package was functioning perfectly you could see things and not understand what you were seeing.

Caroline had wanted to see the flowers of the Queen of the Night but the plant didn't bloom until late in the spring. It was just an inconspicuous stick but when it flowered it was an ethereal sight, you really couldn't enjoy it enough when it flowered. She

had seen it once and she wanted to see it again but spring was too far, too far for her. He'd gone to a nursery and asked if the bloom couldn't be forced and the nurseryman said he didn't think so but he was still learning. He wasn't even a nurseryman yet, just an employee. And he was from back east so he actually knew shit all about the area and its plants. Just the other day he'd been told that spines evolved from leaves and he still didn't know whether to believe it because he'd been told, too, that you couldn't look at a tree and say the name of it at the same time so he suspected they were still hazing him.

Tom never knew if the Queen of the Night he'd bought had ever flowered. Some years they don't. Sometimes sticks stay sticks.

The ironwood box had been broken open surely. Had the thief possessed the decency to inter the ashes in an appropriate manner or dispose of them with ceremony on the wind over a great sea?

It was unlikely.

He struck his knee viciously, accidentally, against the fish tank and limped outside, into the enervated light.

The resort had several pools, none of them functional. Honey preferred the one filled with specific trash—paintings, furniture, broken bottles—for her training. The rooms here had been filled with art, but the canvases were in fragments now and the colored shards of glass snapped and shone among them. She adored training. Training and exclaiming:

Democratically approved protest is doomed!
Legitimate murder is no match for illegitimate mayhem.

She loved giving herself over to training and exclaiming much as she had loved donating blood or getting baptized. She'd been baptized a dozen times. She'd become a little compulsive about

it, she guessed. Pentecostal storefronts, burby churches, white Congoed steepled establishments, cavernous Baptist temples . . . in all she had been welcomed and received, desperately in some cases. She liked whatever—the water poured, daubed, rubbed or sprinkled from silver fonts or humble bowls—but she preferred dips in octagonal pools or full immersion in "natural" bodies of water. Her baptism in a river, which she had so excitedly antici- pated, proved to be her last, however, when she found she simply could not ignore the scrap of turquoise carpet floating past, the snaggle of brush and rope and plastic jugs, even a ragged fleecy leg pointing straight to heaven.

There goes the devil, a flame-haired, sopping wet boy observed, pointing at the cloven hoof, and seemed quite pleased.

After that, though Honey was hardly a cleanliness freak, she tried to fulfill her sacral needs through giving blood. She had just wanted to give and give. But then someone told her that they really didn't need as much blood as they were always calling for and they ended up throwing half of it away, either from careless- ness or because it had expired. There was an expiration date for everything. And *then* someone told her that blood mostly went to the super wealthy who depended upon frequent transfusions for mental acuity, increased sexual drive and renewal of unequivocally ruthless behavior in the service of making more money. Blood transfusions were tremendously rejuvenating and less supersti- tious than ingesting powdered rhino horn.

Honey had been greatly disturbed by this information but it had been difficult to curtail her donations. She had to slowly wean herself from giving blood. She was like a diver sipping air—or whatever it is that they sip—coming up, rising from the unnatural element of deprivation, rising slowly so as to avoid the niggles and the bends, the chokes and the staggers, to avoid ultimately, death on the greasy boards of the lurching vessel, floating waver-

ingly above. She felt mean like a hoarder—she was hoarding her own blood.

This was why she'd taken up extreme training. Training wasn't everyone's dish of sherbet. Actually no one trained here the way she did but she did not hold this against them. Once she'd asked Hector if he'd ever given blood and he replied that he could not because his blood was too blue. She thought that was a riot. Hector was crazy but so courteous. He never asked about the tunnel like mean old Scarlett. *Should I take the tunnel then?* Scarlett was always asking when of course there was no tunnel, Honey was quite sure. She believed more in a kind of bridge.

*The bridge will appear when you cross it!*

She just hoped she wouldn't have to go through the hospital again. It wasn't just that she owed them so much money. It was the questions, God, the questions they'd asked her.

*What's your favorite territory?*

*The sea*, she'd said.

*Ahh, the sea. The world's heartbreaking beauty will remain when there is no heart to break for it.*

*Or perhaps a little sheltered beach by the sea*, she'd amended. *Like a cove.*

*We want to manage your pain. But we can't help you if you don't believe in us.*

*What do you want me to believe*, she'd said.

*In us.*

Oh she hoped she wouldn't have to pass through that place again.

She moved back and forth across the mess in the pool, her movements something between tai chi and a tango. She could devote herself to the struggle against her very human condition

for hours. She never cut her feet on the glass now. Her feet were hard as horn.

She saw Tom inching his way toward a chair under a collapsing cabana. She waited until he had settled himself, then called out pleasantly, "Many times I think I was born for this!" Not sure of his acknowledgment, she added, "This place."

After a moment he said, "You were, of course."

"It makes me so happy to know our deaths are going to count." There was no reason to think Gordon was right. Why should she trust him with her happiness?

"Yeah," Tom said. "It's nice all right."

"It's like giving God something He doesn't have. A gift, a real gift."

"If He doesn't have it, He probably doesn't need it," Tom said.

"That's so funny! You're right, I mustn't take myself too seriously. The only weird thing will be dying in a crowd after living alone for so long, responsible only to myself and then being responsible for so many, waking them up and then extinguishing them at the same time." She clambered out of the pool and arranged herself beside him. "I have absolutely no horror of dying. One can only have a horror of dying in a world that has invited one to live."

"Yeah," Tom said. "Where is that invitation anyway? I was told to expect it anytime." He mimed distress, confusion, as he paddled at the pocket of his shirt, searching.

"We wouldn't want to be invited now," Honey said worriedly. "But imagine receiving a proper invitation, on nice stationery, heavy cream-colored stationery . . . *you are cordially invited . . .*"

"We got one once but we lost it," Tom said. "What we've been waiting for is the replacement invitation."

"Like a passport. My passport was stolen and when I applied for another one the picture they took wasn't of me at all. So I decided I didn't want one."

Tom covered his left eye and squinted into the distance, then moved his hand to his right eye. Was one not quite so sick? Yes, the left, not so bad. It takes triangular eyes to see heaven, the Russians say.

"You know where I wanted to travel? Russia! Isn't that funny? You spent a lot of time there, didn't you? Tell me about the Russians, they're very soulful, aren't they. What do they talk about?"

"Good and evil," Tom granted her. "Death and the mother."

"Yes, yes, I knew it!" Honey studied him. He was a good-looking man with a pasty complexion and a crease on one side of his head as though someone had gone in there once and taken something out though it might be that the crease could be nothing more than an illusion caused by a bad haircut.

"You did a lot of damage in a professional capacity over there, didn't you," Honey said. "My damage was in the unprofessional line. I just took up space. An increasing amount of space. You could say I had a kind heart, heart of gold but so what. I wasn't the kind of being the earth required and I could tell you the exact moment I realized I wasn't the kind of being the earth required."

Tom dropped his hands from his face. He wanted her to describe the moment, this interested him. He could not tell her the moment when he realized this about himself because he had ignored it. He had put much effort into the many days thereafter, ignoring it. That effort became his life.

"When was the moment you realized?" he finally said.

She sighed. "I told you already. I just told you."

"What are your plans now?" he asked. Had she told him that as well? He felt there was something familiar about what was coming next.

"I'm going to destroy Phoenix."

"Oh yeah," Tom said. "They never should have named it that. Or put it where they did."

"They just hijacked a lovely story and for what? To give name to a stinking metropolis."

He agreed it was an outrage.

"When the creature the Phoenix realizes it is growing old, it builds a funeral pyre of branches and by turning its body toward the sun it beats its wings until it burns up," Honey recounted dreamily. "And then it rises again from the ashes. Nine days, I think. Nine days later it comes back good as new."

"That part's a little sketchy."

"Sometimes the creature builds its own coffin, lies down in it and just dies. Still, the result is the same."

"Took a lot of nerve to call that place Phoenix," he said again, more or less.

"The Hohokum were there first, for a century and more, but then mysteriously vanished. *Hohokum* means all used up or departed. And that's what's going to happen to the Phoenicians, too, do you agree?"

"Absolutely," Tom said. "Replicability and repeatability are scientific facts."

"I love it when they say these sophisticated prehistoric civilizations 'mysteriously vanished.' What do they take us for?"

"Fools. They take us for fools."

"They flaunt their stolen water. They have fountains there which is criminal!"

"Fountains, freeways, the seat of government, an inefficient sewage treatment plan, a vast and smug population, the whole ball of wax."

"They're going to think it was an act of God but it's going to be an act of Honey."

"They'll never see you coming."

"That is so nice of you to say! Do you know the legal definition of an act of God? It's something which no reasonable person could have expected."

"Hadn't heard that one."

"A little kid told me that."

"No reasonable beings anymore, no acts of God either."

"He's an odd little kid. I just saw him once, but I think he's still here. Though he shouldn't be, this is no place for him."

"No place for children of any stripe."

"Children should not be instructed in the suicide arts," Honey mused. "But then again, why not? Ideally, it should just be part of their education. Most school textbooks . . . don't get me started."

"Think I'll head back to my room," Tom said wearily.

"You want me to help you?"

"I've become an old man, afraid of falling," he said in wonder.

"If we weren't operating out of this blessed place, we'd just die of our disabilities. I've heard that Gordon will be giving out little paper scrolly things if our capabilities have changed." She hesitated. "Has he given one to you?"

"Little paper scrolly things?"

"He's determined to shoo us out of this place. He said, I think he was quoting somebody, it sounds a little old-fashioned, he said, 'We are tenants at will of this clayey farm, not for any term of years. The condition of our entrance was finally to depart.' Do you remember him saying that?"

"Uhmm," Tom said.

"Has he given one to you?" she asked again hesitantly. She pictured the paper of a quality similar to one in a fortune cookie, though lacking the fortune's disarming shell.

"Not yet."

"Your original intention was so heroic. It's a shame."

"Overly ambitious. Needs a younger person to implement."

"Well we have to live in the now. To be anywhere other than the now is to paint eyeballs on chaos."

"Good God!" Tom exclaimed.

She blushed. What an inconsiderate thing to say to a person of failing sight! "That was some crazy thing I heard once," she said hurriedly. "It made an impression on me but I've never understood it."

He laughed and she felt happy again.

"You can leave with me before Gordon gives you the little paper scrolly thing," she suggested. "We'd look harmless twice over. They don't expect people like us to turn on them. That's our advantage. They don't expect us to care."

Tom didn't want to make his exit with Honey. "The shit list is long," he said. "I'll find an alternative."

"The shit list is so long! I had lots of first choices. I wanted to strike a blow for the aquatics but their situation made me so sad I couldn't think clearly whereas with Phoenix, it was easy to be coldly focused."

He slowly rose to his feet. "My eyes have adjusted some. I can make my own way."

"Well we all have to, but here, take advantage, you won't have me here tomorrow." She snared his hand in hers. It was large and soft and surprising as a boxing glove.

"The sense of imminent revolution is very strong," Honey said. "I can smell it in the air."

He could not. He could smell that dreadful lake if he so allowed. Deposited at his door, he felt like a child who had been ushered across a dangerous intersection, naturally against his will.

"This was the finest final day I could have hoped for," Honey said. "I suspected I'd be alone, feeling anxious, clumsy, not up to the challenge . . ."

"I feel better too," he lied.

"Though I kind of wish I'd seen that girl, that Khristen girl again," she said honestly.

⌒⌒

All night Tom lay awake.

To see is to forget the name of the thing you see.

That's what the foolish nurseryman had been told and misre-
membered when Tom had gone to him seeking the Queen of the
Night.

Now, against his will he remembered the priest his wife had
insisted upon and the priest was odious and familiar, as was to be
expected. He had said, "The soul cannot be possessed of the divine
union until it has divested itself of the love of all created beings."
He attributed this to St. John of the Cross. He urged her to let go,
let go, that was the ticket.

When the man left, Caroline said with her last strength, "I
can't do that, Tom. I love you. I love everything we had together."

He'd held her hands and kissed them. The truth was that he
had divested himself of loving, even his dear Caroline, long ago
and nothing had happened, nothing had changed. Nothing. It had
even frightened him a little.

He rose from his bed and opened the door to the night. It was
stifling, inside and out. He was on the ground floor. He shuffled
to the edge of the strip of buckled concrete and peed into the dirt.
The few drops he managed made no sound yet a playful breeze
nudged him with a brief and acrid stink. Behind him, the door to
his room gaped open uninvitingly, as did the door beside it. This
was Grayson's room. The shabby chorister, once so desperate for
conversation. He had wanted to talk about religion and exchange
crosses, which was right out of Dostoevsky certainly, Myshkin,
the virtuous idiot, so good he was easily destroyed by others. Tom
was pleased to make the connection though he had had no crosses
to exchange save for the most metaphorical ones.

Grayson no longer seemed to be in residence, however.

Every room had been occupied when he first arrived and the
turnover had been brisk. They were a gabby seditious lot, in the
worst of health but with kamikaze hearts, an army of the aged and

ill, determined to refresh, through crackpot violence, a plundered earth. He was probably the most skilled at mayhem of the lot, his life's work aimed at eliminating the eliminators, or those who were perceived to be the eliminators, but that was the old, coolly rational way.

His Russian friends could go all weepy over the first sticky buds of spring, the tender leaves unfurling, and then direct their considerable energies to creating mayhem and disease.

How morbidly merry they had been. If he'd stayed over there he certainly would have found himself at the mercy of events. "We are at *the mercy of events*," he'd slur of an evening to his good-natured associates, always a reliable guffaw getter. He would have poisoned himself with alcohol by now, or frozen to death.

How they loved their germs. You had to raise them responsibly, as you would a child. Protect them, keep them from becoming precocious too soon. These were germs too nuanced to kill. Why kill when one can dis-create the fundamentals? It had occupied him deeply to horse around in such a way, raising "the kids," the germ events, the bastard rascals.

Toward the east he sensed something struggling to make its appearance, the ashy-fingered dawn no doubt—a new day, departure day—and was reminded of Gordon's commanding paper scrolls. Did they even exist? It seemed a little theatrical, a little party favorish. Honey could well have misheard or misinterpreted something in passing. Eyeballs on chaos after all . . . He wondered if she had left. Did she have any idea how far Phoenix was? She'd be lucky to make a klick on those swollen pins.

"Hallooo . . ."

Tom startled violently. His vision cleared for an instant and there was Gordon in all his awfulness.

"Hear that you're going blind," Gordon said companionably.

"Yes, I . . . The deterioration in the last few days has been . . ."

"Pretty dramatic I bet."

"Sorry to be so slow in getting that out," Tom said.

"From that which I do not see an endless world arises."

Tom said nothing.

"It's all just electrical impulses," Gordon said. "Rods and cones transforming light into waves. The waves carry data through the optic nerve to the brain whereupon the brain forms images. So it is that we actually see not with the eyes but with the brain. Just a technicality."

"Would you like to sit down somewhere?" Tom asked. His legs suddenly felt shaky.

"Sure. In your room? Sit on your bed if that's all right?"

"Yes," Tom said.

"Where is it?"

"What."

"Your bed."

"Oh," Tom said.

"OK then," Gordon said. "So you no longer find this place to your liking anymore? This place of preparation for a meaningful death that would provide redress?"

Dawn was moving with graceless haste into bright day. It was hot. Gordon was wearing a coat, perhaps to protect his skin. The coat was darkly florid, preposterous.

"I wanted to provide redress," Tom admitted.

"For a life poorly lived . . . Do you remember a group called Friends of the Earth, Tom? FOE?"

"Yes, I tried to contact them shortly before I arrived. I had a lot of information that could be modified to their approach. But they'd gone underground. I couldn't find them."

"Underground?!" Gordon shrieked. "They were erased! Thoughtful, selfless, beautiful people, really. The last of the true advocates. FOE, what a pathetic acronym for a group so unformidable. Underground," he giggled. "Actually it's true, you weren't being misled."

"I didn't know. I thought they were still active but not as . . . as visible."

"Post-FOE, there's the terrible trinity. The relativists, the survivalists and groups of filthy youth who think they can still save the earth by grinding up some modest nut or bean for pancake meal. Have you ever had one of their goddamn proselytizing pancakes?"

"I don't believe I have."

"They make cooking fires of turds. But even those poor clowns are being denied permits. And without a permit, they're not even allowed a good cry."

"Who issues the permits?"

"The minister of energy," Gordon giggled. "The minister of energy handles pretty much everything now. You have to pity the fools who still want to recycle their toothbrushes and plant apple trees. Let them turn the lights off or never turn them on, it can't matter now. They were inoculated against bringing down the system with their toddler shots."

"What I need to know," Tom said, "rather what I would appreciate knowing, is why you came back. I didn't think we were supposed to come back. We were supposed to leave and engage— throw our spoiling carcasses on the earth's wounds while taking out a couple of bastards."

"We're pulling the plug here, Tom. You've waited too long. If you're allowed a few moments of perception when you leave you'll find that the aged and dying are once again reduced to being only laughably feisty or touchingly grateful or predictably demented or whiningly fuddled."

"I've heard that you're going to give us an ultimatum."

There was an odd smell, like earth untouched beneath a pleasant porch.

"I spoke with Grayson earlier. Nice little fellow. Quiet. Anti-

triumphant. Terrible procrastinator though. When he finally un-wrapped what I gave him, he said, 'Whose handwriting is this?' Somewhere he was encouraged to believe that irrelevant inquiry is a successful parry."

"What was it? Did he accept?"

"Oh he had no choice. It was a good one. Womb banks."

"What are they?" Tom said cautiously.

"His next question exactly. They're harvesting wombs from brain-dead donors to have on hand for uterine transplants. Fertility doctors want to offer their patients more opportunities. They're inspired by those women who want the experience of pregnancy even if they have to borrow a dead girl's womb. Another remarkable example of civilization unraveled, in irreversible decline. By hitting a bunch of womb storage facilities Grayson will be side-swiping at least one aspect of the irresponsible future."

"It doesn't seem . . ."

"His was a life of uncreative solitude. Who knows what he would have chosen for himself. It was never clear. Anyway, after a bit he pulled himself together and went off caroling something or other. Terrible voice."

Tom's eyes burned behind his glasses. But when he raised his hand to remove them he couldn't locate them. "Do you happen to see my glasses about?"

"I do. Here they are."

He felt Gordon's fingers which were rough and wet, and shrank away.

"You probably don't need them but if they make you feel more comfortable . . ."

"You're right. No. Don't need them," Tom said.

"Have you ever reflected on what earth's advance directive would be, Tom?"

"I'm ashamed to say, no."

"You think she'd want treatment even if there were no cure? Even if treatment only ensured that her dying would be more prolonged? Or do you think she'd ask for comfort care only?"

"I'd say it was just as well the earth didn't entrust us with a directive," Tom said. "She shouldn't have entrusted us with anything."

"Nature's too innocent, no match against our designs. Anyone who's served their country as long as you have knows that to be true."

"I did what was asked of me," Tom said. "I drew the line at doing more."

"Quite a rebellious constitution you've got."

"I'm detestable, I wish I could be punished."

"But you're not going to be," Gordon said piously. "Not really."

"I'm no longer sure I know what this place is. I thought I did. When I found it, I felt I'd kicked myself up a rung, that a fresh destiny would be mine and I would be serving good, not a superficial good, but something deep, a good incomprehensible to conditioned minds."

Gordon laughed. "That's what you thought you were doing before. And now you think you imagined this place? The possibility it afforded you? The second chance?" He pushed his hand into the pocket of his overcoat.

Tom realized that what Honey had called a little paper scrolly thing was about to be delivered. It was undoubtedly nothing he would have chosen but he had never chosen wisely or well. There was the familiar yet strange smell again, desirable and dangerous. Time was withdrawing from him, Tom could feel it. Still, there was enough time remaining to wonder how Gordon could withstand the heaviness of that coat, for the day had become warm, the heat was ungodly really, a tenor of heat that on those steppes that

had comprised so much of his life caused the shepherd dogs to go mad and tear all the lambs they lived to guard to pieces.

The place didn't appear to Khristen to be any more decrepit than usual but a silence had fallen over everything. It was the wind, she thought. The wind had ceased and with it the appearance of movement, of life. The meeting in Laundery had sounded some closing note and everyone had scattered as though a dark predator had arrived.

She wandered the ruined web of the resort's grounds. Many of the buildings' wings had burned, leaving enormous charred timbers. The ground, too, was charred shadow. She remembered a bit of fencing where sunflower stalks leaned, their great seedless heads drooping, but she could no longer locate it. Things were always revealing and concealing themselves here. She felt she was undergoing a test she could not pass. Still, it all felt irretrievably familiar. Could this possibly have been the site of the conference her mother had attended in hopes of being part of the new thinking, in hopes of hearing the delivering word? But it had only been weeks, months at the most, since Khristen had left the school, and her mother had disappeared not long before that. Yet it had been years, many years possibly, since this place had been functioning, decaying even before the life outside it had collapsed.

She tried to imagine her mother here, listening to the utterances of fine minds. *Daily existence is a falling into the inauthentic.* Some fine mind came up with that. A dead mind, though the thoughts lived, the words. Appearing unsummoned. You listen to the dead with your eyes.

But there was no daily existence here. Nor could it possibly be authentic. If this had been the place her mother had denied everything to reach, she had arrived just before all of it was bro-

ken, when the finest minds still preached control and possession, adaptation and modification. Khristen had arrived to see it now, in ruins, the concert pavilions, the lecture halls, the gymnasiums and meditation chambers—the roofless library where the massive books slouched on broad shelves, rippled as though made of lead, their pages sealed, irretrievable.

Khristen would never locate a memory of her mother here. This was not a place of retrieval, of recognition. She would leave this place, as she had left her situation at the school before it and the situation before that, which ended the morning after her father's death, when she had waited, all illusions of known home dissolved, watching a screen within which a bird, with futile care, turned an egg over and over in a nest of sticks. She remembered being given a glass of water while she waited and it slipped from her grasp and as the glass fell she, too, fell into a long moment and when she emerged from that moment, the glass had yet to smash to pieces upon the floor with the accompanying cry of surprise and dismay.

It is in such a moment where the dead reside, forever.

She could have offered her mother that. It is like Death is the long moment outside the smash-up that is life.

She passed the sunflowers with their dark averted faces. There they were! She had never gotten her bearings on these broken grounds. She would have been an inadequate guide certainly had Lola employed her in that fashion. But that was a suggestion that had been made only once and Khristen had not again seen the truck she'd driven here, the old professor's truck.

She moved into a small clearing which afforded a glimpse of the hotel. She had not wandered far from it at all. On the ground flickered something golden. It was a scorpion. She knelt to see it more clearly and saw six more.

The lake was behind her. Honey thought it was funny, well, horrible actually, that Lola called it Big Girl. In the beginning she tried to do what Lola did—go down to its shores in the evening when the sand was quick, it really was, almost, and say, "I love you, Big Girl!" which Honey felt was a bit like fervently addressing a corpse though she wouldn't dream of saying that to Lola. She could almost believe that something was down there, some patron goddess, in retreat from a world from which the sacred had withdrawn. Her significance was contradictory, that was for sure. Now, with distance, she could even perceive Big Girl as a vast baptismal bowl. It only made sense that the waters of renewal in these dreadful times would have to be a little strange, even abhorrent, and certainly not inviting. Submergence should be fearsome, initiation an ordeal, ordination a grim awakening! Big Girl was perfect. After that meeting in Laundery they all should have entered her together, arms linked, a singing chain. Oh it would have been nice! It was important to see what things really were. That filthy river of her other life had been telling her one thing and she had heard something else entirely. She had not understood that river. She had denied it.

She rather wished she had stayed at the Institute, sharing this insight with others, entering Big Girl with joy. Wasn't that what such a presence was for—a mystery to approach and be received?

No. She didn't know what Big Girl was for. Even the gaunt clouds that had attended the lake in nightly vigil seemed uncertain.

In any case, she was outside the Institute now. She'd really done it, there was no going back.

She was passing beneath enormous windmills. The great blades advertising pharmaceuticals were still. They were probably still a lot, locked in place. Otherwise the drug companies wouldn't be getting their money's worth by sponsoring them.

When Honey was sixteen, a girl who was sixteen as well told them, all of them sixteen, sweet sixteen, that when a man and a

woman are making a baby, if the sperm gets in there a second before or a second after, an entirely different person is made, the genes will be different. Seconds, minutes, hours, it makes a difference in who you are that you will never be aware of, the girl told them, that you couldn't possibly know.

We know you're nuts, one of them said. Jeans like Levi's? You're an idiot.

No one believed anything that girl said. Later she drank antifreeze at a Halloween party and died. She'd told everyone she was going to drink it but no one believed her. Honey had always been a little attracted to her. She'd wished she'd kissed her when she could have, earlier.

The blades of one of the windmills moved fractionally and then stopped. The names of the drugs on the blades were unbeautiful. Honey had never heard of them, they were a new generation of drugs.

The girl had swirled the liquid in the glass like she was a connoisseur of the stuff and then she drank it.

Honey hadn't thought of that girl, or the wishing she had kissed her when she could have, in ages.

Oh she remembered terrible things. Sad things. She wanted to remember the happy now.

Once, after Honey had given blood, a pretty nurse had said to her in all seriousness, "We don't want you to ride in fast elevators for the next twenty-four hours," and Honey had said, "I don't know any fast elevators."

Those days were fun. Honey always looked at the blood they'd taken, that she'd *given*, she'd twist around on the rubbery bed they made you lie on and regard it. It was beautiful. And it was not a simple thing. Of its three precious components, all three were useful but plasma might be the best, for it treated shock. It was required for organ transplants, too, she knew. There were Packed

Red Cells, Platelet Concentrate and Plasma. Platelet Concentrate was good for hemorrhage.

It was always strangers who got her blood. She never directed her donations like some people. Some people had a particular individual in mind. Or some people specified babies, just babies. Their blood went into special bags, just pediatric use. But your blood had to be O for the babies.

The underlying assumption in giving blood was that the invisible ones, the unknown ones who received it, were necessary. But that was a false assumption. They were not necessary. No one was necessary. This awareness was Honey's evolvement. Once evolvement occurred, you saw the world differently and that was that.

Now she wasn't sure whether the evolvement had occurred before she'd learned that prominent and powerful people purchased gallons of blood just to refresh themselves, or after. Or perhaps she hadn't stopped giving blood by her own volition at all but because she'd been forbidden to. She'd been placed on a list of people forbidden.

Yet those early days had been so nice. After the pint was drawn she could have donuts, orange juice, crackers. Occasionally there were free movie tickets. T-shirts as well were sometimes given in gratitude. She'd had some good ones though none better than the last which had been her favorite even before she knew it was the last.

LIFE IS UNPREDICTABLE, THE NEED FOR BLOOD IS NOT

It depicted a happy-go-lucky fellow lounging on a beach float in the ocean. An island with a palm tree nearby. Under the float, a shark, jaws agape.

LIFE IS UNPREDICTABLE, THE NEED FOR BLOOD IS NOT

She mumbled this as she plodded along but soon it gave her no pleasure. On reflection it was imprecise. How could it be the case that the need for blood was predictable? She could very well envision a world where the need for blood was beside the point. There was blood and then there were the methods by which the blood was administered. Disrupt the methods of delivery and what have you got? Plastic baggies of trembling red fluid that had to be refrigerated and had an expiration date.

The windmills were behind her and she was passing through a shabby community of roofless houses. People were sitting on porches watching her. Honey paused by a little piece of turned earth, the remains of a garden, and labored to breathe. She should have considered this—she really couldn't walk far, it was like walking on footballs. Her training was useless out here. Her poor feet, she couldn't even see them.

A figure slowly hitched itself up from a rocking chair and waved a shotgun at her. She supposed the figure was human. The wind tossed his words away from her then tossed them back.

*Get away from them tomatoes.*

On the ridge, the wind was avoiding the inhospitable windmills, their club-like blades of fiercest white. It tore, unharnessed, about the valley instead.

*Get away you.*

*You.*

*From them tomatoes.*

Honey wore a poncho that grasped and scratched at her flesh when she raised a hand in greeting.

The people on the porch were openly staring at her. There were more than there had been, creeping out from around and beneath the house, from the adumbrated dark there. The building was in need of repair, every aspect of it. Even the harrow painted on the door was in need of a touch-up. Perhaps if she offered her assistance they would give her a morsel to eat. She had to

eat something. A single tomato was all it would take to keep her going.

She stood by the little plot. The earth was gray and the fruit was small and misshapen. She reached out her hand and an astonishing pain ripped through it. Her arm was sheared from her body, and then she felt her great breasts being flayed, ripped in strips like you would do to bundles of old sheets to provide for something or someone in an emergency situation.

Her whole life. It was as though it hadn't happened yet, or had, and had been forgotten and replaced with only this.

Khristen wanted to tell Lola about the scorpions. This didn't seem to be their natural habitat though nothing seemed to be moving through a natural habitat anymore.

The great door to the hotel's lobby was open, indeed it seemed to have been partially torn from its hinges. She could just make out, within, a chair upon which the old man sat, the old woman perched like a child upon his lap.

"Hello, dear," Lola said.

She looked dreadful, decrepit. Her few little sprigs of hair lay flat against her skull.

"Jeffrey and his mother have left. Were you able to say goodbye? I told her she shouldn't drive in her condition but she ignored me of course. She left the place spotless however. I was surprised."

"Grebe," Khristen said.

"Why yes! I remember those birds only faintly. They never laughed like their brothers and sisters, the loons." She coughed for a moment in a violent fashion. "We're going soon too. You mustn't leave with us but you can't stay here."

"She could stay here," the old man offered. "She could study the humanities. Pry open those books, bury herself alive in them."

"Gordon's all bark," Lola said. "He's the one who devoted himself to the humanities for years in one of those idyllic preparatory schools with the bell towers, the chapel, the courts of clay . . ."

"We were reminiscing just before you arrived," Gordon said. "I'm in your debt actually. You kept old Lola going until I could get back. Perhaps you will be rewarded. Though it's possible you won't be rewarded at all. Pull up a chair."

"These two chairs have been in my life since I was a little girl," Lola said. "I was never allowed to sit on them so I pretended they were electric chairs. What fascination they held for me!"

"When our great inventors were first indulging in this execution frolic, they tested the voltage on elephants," Gordon said.

Khristen had not seen these chairs before. Everything here was poorly mended or merely broken, but these were intact. "You brought these from your childhood?" she wondered.

"Oh no, dear," Lola said.

"Sit down then," Gordon said. "It's sturdy. Could accept two or three of you. As I said, we were reminiscing, discussing the little contest that took place long before you were born. I was in the aforementioned prestigious school. My classmates and I were groomed for success. Encouraged to hammer down absolute distinctions between man, nature and the supernatural. Going strong for two hundred years, then we lose the contest and it was irrelevancy for us within six months."

"It rankles him still. But Gordon, you must admit, yours was not an original submission."

"We were traditionalists."

"Tell the story to Khristen. She'll appreciate it."

"I was fifteen in that excellent institution. Lola was a mere five, in a distant kindergarten."

"I'm ten years younger than Gordon and always will be," Lola said with satisfaction.

"The government was sponsoring a contest which all schools were encouraged to enter. The challenge was to design a symbol for nuclear depositories, weapons cemeteries, sterile spaces. Only the younger generations could work on it. It was all very hush-hush. Delivering the perfect ideogram would have been enormously prestigious. Winning would secure our school's reputation as the great incubator of our country's leaders for yet another two hundred years. We were so confident, so certain of our supremacy in pretty much every endeavor that we felt that coming up with an image that would indicate that certain vast tracts of the planet had been poisoned by human endeavor for all eternity and should never be approached would be a piece of cake. That the image's message, as we understood the guidelines, should be elliptical yet direct, that its immediate effect on the viewer should be devastating yet not annihilative to the human spirit—that is, while instilling fear, it would avoid eliciting panic—was also not beyond our patriotic powers. We were confident because this school, our school, bred us to prevail. We knew we would win. But we didn't win. We lost."

"It looked much like a sea star," Lola said. She looked so small on Gordon's lap, wearing her faded dress. He wore a fulsome coat which revealed only his weeping hands and face. Scaly, speckled, very awful, as the chorister had noted.

With the nail of his index finger, Gordon drew in the dust on the table.

"A sea star!" Khristen exclaimed. She remembered them on a shelf, mummified, with shells and the dried jaws of fishes.

"That was our entry. Instead the contest was won by a bunch of kidlets who didn't even have their feathers yet, a common

primary school class. Lola's. She was in the winner's circle even then."

"But winning became losing, Gordon, as you are well aware," Lola said. "Upon further consideration, the government did not find our submission appropriate to their intentions and the prize was rescinded. The Awards Committee was discredited and the hounding of our little group began. We were monitored constantly. We were not allowed to share snacks, we were forbidden to paint. They took away our pretty snakes and our monk parrot. Just busted in and put their fists in his cage and took him away. They said he was not native to the region. 'Marvelous is a good boy, Marvelous is a good boy,' he kept saying to no avail. Off he was taken to quarantine and certain death. They burnt our desks and forced our teacher out. They rescinded her certificate. She fled to the Great Desert and endured several ruthless winters. The winters were screaming fierce, it was just beginning then. We kept in feral contact at first. 'Why don't you leave?' we'd say, meaning why don't you come back. 'Leave,' she'd say, 'Why it's all I can do to stay.'"

Both Lola and Gordon chuckled at this.

"She was a visionary, that dumpy dear playground monitor, but only that once. The annunciatory image announced itself to her and she shared it with us. We set aside our usual materials, the popsicle sticks and uncooked macaroni, the glitter and flour and glycerol, and turned to the task of a lifetime. How happy we were then, how industrious."

"At least they didn't starve you pups. In the old days if your election was overturned your political opponents would starve you to death. Your sons as well. And your grandsons. Daughters and granddaughters it goes without saying. Many would like the custom reinstated."

"Can you tell me what it was, the sign you made?" Khristen asked Lola.

"The Tao that can be named is not the true Tao," Gordon giggled. "The Tao that can be named . . . Goodness, I wish I could wipe tears of laughter from my eyes." To Khristen, he said, "Their winning entry was babyish. It was exactly what you might expect from a pod of carelessly indoctrinated little children. It was an ark. A comically familiar ark."

"But the ark was empty," Lola said. "Myriad creatures were present but they were below the vessel, supporting it. The ark was no longer protecting them, they were protecting the ark. Behind this centerpiece was a charred earth, before it, a chalky blankness."

"That's the part the authorities misinterpreted," Gordon said. "They saw what lay ahead as a clean slate where human ingenuity could play and prosper and provide. A new frontier."

"Others saw the chalky fog as a fathomless depth of ignorance, apathy and the inadequacy of response."

"When the disparity of perception was noted there was . . . concern," Gordon said.

"In many regards, we were meticulously by the book. The ark had three decks, three stories, and there was but one window and one door. But there were absences that made them uneasy. The ark lacked the sea. We children had failed to provide the squiggles."

"The squiggles," Gordon said delightedly. "The lack of squiggles made the prize givers increasingly suspicious. How could such innocent hands and hearts be so sly, so susceptible to nihilism!"

"In the end," Lola said, "the dangerous and ever multiplying sequestrums were simply put off limits behind the usual affairs—fences, walls, electric fields, unpleasant lights. They even employed the image offered by Gordon and his crowd for they realized it had just been copied from an Egyptian hieroglyph. What seemed a sea star meant *kingdom of death*."

"We were entitled but lazy," Gordon admitted.

"The design for a permanent danger marker for the future— for future humans—was put on hold, though the original inten-

tion of warning rather than edification was stressed. A blue-ribbon panel was empowered to study the challenge. There were two anthropologists, an archaeologist, an astronomer, two geologists, a linguist and a cognitive psychologist. When one died they cycled in another of the same discipline."

"Future humans, such a reckless concept," Gordon said. "Well, such expertise is unnecessary now. The old thinking has been replaced by the new thinking. The aborted are being adopted in colorful ceremonies and the graveyards are being plowed to plant corn."

"It's so unlike what I had hoped," murmured Lola.

"The hair of the dead is being woven into handy baskets and totes. Everything is being utilized. Only the animals are still mourning the death of their kind. It's become a bit of a sport to watch them grieve."

Khristen suddenly felt the chair crumple beneath her. It wasn't so sturdy after all. She leapt up but looking at it, she saw it was the same, unbroken.

"You must have more faith in yourself, dear," Lola said.

" 'God seeketh again that which is passed away,' " Gordon said, his breath whistling, a dimpled void between the words. "That's what my Lola likes to say and I always agree. He seeketh. But will He findeth?"

"Did the scorpions find you, dear?"

"I saw them," Khristen said. "I meant to tell you."

"But where are they?"

"Outside. They were so golden. I thought it strange."

"They were meant to travel with you, dear."

"Lola's always had a fondness for the minor deities," Gordon said.

Lola sighed. "Would you mind getting us some water, dear. I'm just so tired I don't want to move."

Khristen went to the washroom off the lobby. She inspected the folds of her clothes but they harbored no scorpions. Drops leaked from the little sink's faucet but turning the handle provided nothing more. There were no cups or glasses about. There was nothing to bear the water in at all except her hands.

BOOK THREE

*Why should I have returned?*
*My knowledge would not fit into theirs.*
*I found untouched the desert of the unknown,*
*Big enough for my feet. It is my home.*
*It is always beyond them. The future*
*Splits the present with the echo of my voice.*
*Hoarse with fulfillment, I never made promises.*

"NOAH'S RAVEN"
W. S. MERWIN

*Does God care whether you are living or dead?*

*[. . . . . . . . . . . . . . . . . . . . .]*

*But would that not presume He loves the living more than the dead? And would that not be unendurable for those who had believed in Him?*

His MOTHER HAD CHRISTENED HIM PETERPAUL. SHE THOUGHT both names were pretty, she didn't want to choose. His mother was so . . . she was so . . . hapless.

"You know what they're gonna call me," he said, as soon as he was old enough to figure, "they're gonna call me Pee Pee, Ma."

"There are great churches named PeterPaul," she said, throwing more ingredients into one of her wretched casseroles. She used weed, like parsley, as a garnish. "Whyever would they think of calling you Pee Pee?"

"Have you ever heard the phrase 'robbing Peter to pay Paul,' Ma, have you?" He felt canceled out, a zero.

What a battle it had been, quashing the mockery of his name. He'd had to be ever suspicious and alert and confident. But it was only after the incident, that awful unfair incident with that baby in that unlucky house, that the taunt had at last ceased. No one wanted to refer to him at all. He had become superstitiously nameless.

He wasn't Catholic anymore. He had left the church when his mother died though he lived in the same house they'd always lived in. All of her junk was still there but he'd placed it in one room and closed the door. He'd get around to cleaning it out one day and distributing her effects wisely and rationally—her broken-down shoes, her collection of plastic bangles, her rosaries, ditto her smelly hose, her candy tins. Everything hers was in there. She

herself was in the damp hypogeum in the lee of St. Margaret's, a place with serious drainage issues that the parish left unaddressed and which he was loath to visit.

The very day he buried her he had begun the process to legally change his name to Nolo. You could do just about anything you wanted to if you went through the proper channels. He then began training as a paramedic, a first responder. He liked strong-arming any hysterical family member or friend at the scene, to treat them like criminals which they practically were, for they were alive and their purported loved ones who they were screaming about were damn near not.

He had no respect for the hospital out of which he worked— Mercy—nor for the police, with whom he was frequently paired. *Don't call the cops, call your mother,* the wits said, and concerning Mercy, *First they kill you, then they bill you.*

"Nolo," one of the cops had ventured early on. "Like *nolo contendere?*"

"You got it."

"That's not bad, man. Good positioning. You can't be too careful, right?"

His mother had died of a congested heart, had drowned in her body's own fluids. She hadn't taken care of herself, she'd been foolish and timid, addicted to hope and ginger candies. He never consumed sweets or alcohol, he never prayed or brooded. He lived simply—a futon, a few bowls, boots he took very good care of. He was in excellent physical condition, lean with rage. He ran, often with a thirty-pound pack of rocks on his back. He was solitary and furious. People left him and his mother's broken-down house alone.

He was watching a hockey game with one of his acquaintances, Denver Erie Ford. People had been naming their children after dangerous cities for some time now. Denver claimed to have been the beginning of the trend some thirty years before.

"You were probably conceived there, in the Mile-High City," Nolo said.

"I'm sure I was," Denver agreed, "but the idea's become decadent. Things are cyclic and at the end of the cycle is decadence."

"That sounds right."

"Like you notice the players are all inking Bible verses on their sticks."

"These ones aren't."

"These ones suck," Denver said. "They're leaking oil." He was a 911 operator but he'd been told to kick back, take a break, take a long weekend. "It's not a mile high anymore," he mused. "It shrunk."

"I thought you'd been canned."

"No, no, no, absolutely not, not canned," Denver protested. "They just want me to get some rest. It's a stressful job. Somebody drives their car off the road into a canal and the filthy water's halfway up the windows and you have to keep saying, 'What were the last cross streets you remember?' And you have to speak totally without affect."

"But you lost your total lack of affect, I heard. I believe you said to some frightened caller, 'Disaster can sometimes result in supreme victory.'"

"I'd been reading the great dramatists," Denver said. "I mean the real great dramatists. The Tragedians. They got to me, man."

"Everyone's heard the tape. They're loving it. Woman's having a meltdown and you're saying, 'Calamity is often necessary for rebirth.'"

"Well it is, even for the ladies, though I must admit, the great dramatists don't give the ladies much slack to play hero. The fact remains that spiritual progress often depends upon physical disaster. The hero, surviving this, brings with him into the future a past world for re-creation by a divinity whose nature has been recast during the struggle."

"What struggle?"

"You're not listening. The struggle with circumstances that want to crush him. The messenger arrives. In great tragedies, the other characters have fallen away at the end."

"At the denouement?"

"Yeah, the denouement. That's not the way you pronounce it though. The hero faces the gods alone."

"I think that woman's going to sue you."

"In tragedy, everything has happened before it begins. The messenger appears and relates the circumstances of death, the violence of which is seldom portrayed upon the stage. This in itself is a deliberate rejection of opportunity, theatrical opportunity. The messenger is nobody but he holds all the cards, man." Denver looked at the brawl proceeding in real time on the ice. "Sometimes I just want to kick this fucking screen in."

"Change the channel."

Denver ran through a dozen, stopped, reversed. "I could get killed doing this."

"What!"

"This old movie here. This is a great one, the one where the guy says, 'I could get killed doing this,' and the other guy says, 'You could get killed walking your doggie.' I love this one. Is that your pager?"

Another action by some elderlies on behalf of . . . God only knew what it was on behalf of. The little bit of respect the majority of their ilk had accrued just by being tediously and quietly old had been squandered by these nuts. These people had no moral poise in Nolo's opinion. They were a disgrace.

"You're the messenger," Denver called out to him as he left. "Be the messenger."

There was the usual mayhem. Flames, smoke, the air's bitter tang, some plush and fetid hole of wonder opening up.

"What's this building make, anyway?"

"Baby wipes? Salad bowls? I don't know. Some goddamn switch for some goddamn thing."

"Lots of law enforcement out here."

"They're not telling us anything. Just that there are no other known victims except for these two crazies."

The old woman lay close to the old man, which allowed Nolo as he squatted to address both with ease. "Hey, Grandma," he said to her, "you a follower of Mohammed?" There was no reply and he shook her. "Behold: Mohammed says, 'I went to the gates of hell and it was filled with women. I went to the gates of heaven and it was filled with men.'" He shook her again. "You already passed, but listen, listen to me. I know you can still hear me, that's the way it works, there have been studies. The only women Mohammed allows in heaven are the ones who died in childbirth. You should have taken that into consideration. You missed the great opportunity.

"Hey Pops," he said, turning to the man. "How's it going?"

With a grand unnecessary gesture, he slashed open the old fellow's overcoat which was soft as a bird's breast.

"You could have just unbuttoned it," the old man said.

"No, no, this shows our belief that every second counts, that we did everything we could. But it was a nice coat. Now nobody's going to want it. Your shirt red, Pops? Or is that blood?"

"Blood, I believe."

"I don't know much about medicine, I don't have the patience for it but someone told me this once and it just stuck with me. *Cancer cells are reproductive but not productive.* And this. I like this even better, I think. *Cancer cells are all delayed death and uncontrolled birth.*"

"I don't have cancer."

"No? Well you're very fortunate. But you're not going to see the moon rise, Dad. Your chest cavity is seriously messed up. Why'd you want to blow yourselves up for, you and your haggy

friend? What did you think they were making in that building that you were so disapproving of? Because I heard it was salad bowls. You're not thinking big. Old people never think big. You think about bowels and breakfast, right? Not bowls and breakfast. *Bowels* and breakfast. Let me ask you something while I've got you here. Is healthy shit supposed to float or sink? I can never remember which is best. Better?"

Prattling away, he knelt beside the dying man, carelessly poking at his chest. Enormous tan clouds rolled across the sky and there was the familiar sound of thunder that brought no rain.

"What's with your skin anyway? This sort of putrid is not the result of this evening only. You've been using the wrong kind of moisturizer. My guess is you were dipping into the paint remover instead of the cocoa butter." He knelt beside him, sometimes yelling for *a little frigging assistance,* knowing the situation was beyond all medical intervention.

No one cared about these depressed and misguided elderlies, both dead now. Theirs was not a tragic situation. They were not civilized, no longer even human. Civilization was important. He was all for it. Terrorist assaults on factories and institutions, no matter how deleterious their products and convictions might be, ate away at the very fabric of civilization.

From the dead man's pocket, he extracted a small leaf of paper tied incomprehensibly with thread.

When I returned from the anteroom, the water Lola sought having slipped through my fingers, she and Gordon had vanished. For a time I lingered, but the wind seemed furious that there was no one to address but me and eventually turned me out.

The world outside the ravaged Institute was not immediately unfamiliar to me though little I'd been told prepared me for the first day without my old people, my familiars. They were flawed

and their efforts futile, but living among them when the apocalypse had come and gone, scrubbing the world of grief and love, was what I had been given to know. They had hoped to awaken others, but perhaps we are not meant to awake. Perhaps it is only death's long instant that arouses us from sleep.

The day was bright, of a boiling intensity. The cataclysmic had been absorbed. Multitudes pressed past me, eager to inhabit a world that would suffice, where emptiness would not be perceived as emptiness. The creatural companions of childhood, even then glimpsed only in zoos and aquariums, would no more have existed here than the griffins and dragons imagined by the ancients.

I passed a theater, derelict behind a chain-link fence, the triangular wire entwined with dead vines. The theater had been called, was still called THE HOUR, the letters bright as bone. Everyone had a theater like this, in which life went so puzzlingly by, but this had been mine, and it was closed to me, this life was now closed to me.

Beyond The Hour was a park, or a town square, with a single tree, so massive and old that it seemed to me that it had quite forgotten about dying, much like the tree of my youth that believed it would live forever and so inspired the wrath of people. I dimly heard the sea of my infancy, the sound of its waves rolling the rocks as it sought the shore which was not its home, seeking and finding and leaving the shore, again and again. My infancy . . . a void of dark and voices wordless, and my heart as though bridled, being led forward.

I approached the tree and saw a figure attending to it with great concentration. He held a file. Already a bit of the rough, grooved bark was torn.

"Civilians can't use power tools," he informed me easily. "They're too noisy. There are ordinances against them."

I could not hear myself remonstrating with him but I heard his replies.

"Not my business to answer why. Ain't nobody's business to."

He poked and pried at the tree with his little file, a vandal working in a semiprofessional capacity.

"We're pioneers," he said, "and pioneers have to be unconventional." He looked upward in the dark branches that blocked out the very sky above us. "This," he said, "is so conventional."

I knelt and brushed the scraps of crumpled bark into my hand. It burned, it was searing, and I dropped it. My palm was reddened. In a few moments I could not even bend my fingers or make a fist. But it no longer hurt.

"No no," he said. "You don't do that now. You don't know anything, do you? This is a big undertaking and it don't like it that it's found itself to be an undertaking, it don't like us. Now don't suck on that hand, you'll get sick. Trees carry disease and they're getting meaner. All sorts of stories of them falling on folks, crushing them. They didn't used to be so nasty when there were more of them. Not like us girls and boys. We don't get nicer the more of us there are. We've exceeded the earth's carrying capacity and that's a wondrous thing. Shows we can do anything."

I picked up the shattered bark and again held it in my hand. It no longer burned.

"You think you're going to tame that or something? It don't matter. Tame or wild it's going down. Your empathies are obsolete. The battle's over, the world's been overcome. Almost everything that's not us or hasn't been fashioned by us is gone. We're free to make our own new innocence now." He feinted at the tree with his file, stabbed it once, then returned the file to his pocket. "Where'd you come from? If you come from away you'd best go to the courthouse first. Check in as a courtesy. Well it isn't a courtesy exactly, more a requirement. I would think, anyway, you being from away. Though others go there too. I have to tell you they do not have my sympathy. I think they're afraid."

"Where is the courthouse?" I said. Of course I was thinking of Jeffrey and his solemn games.

"Why it's right over there. Right opposite. You can't miss it. Some people say there's a judge in it, just a little fellow, he with whom one has to do, they say. My opinion is he's not a real judge, he's just serving in the capacity of a judge. In any case he's got no right to judge the pioneers." He looked at me impatiently. "I tell you, this area's being cleared, tonight, tomorrow, any minute. You can't stay here."

"I've heard that," I said.

He nodded.

"I've heard that before," I said.

He scowled at me and stepped away.

Jeffrey was indeed a judge, he had not been thwarted in his aim and he appeared much as he had at the age of ten. His slim, even frail figure was engulfed in the robes he wore.

Usually he would present two similar pictures enlarged upon a screen in his courtroom and say to a frightened defendant, "What are the differences here? There are four. Can you find them?"

The picture was of a man and woman looking at a boat in its cradle in a winter shipyard. A sea was in the distance. There were shrouds on some of the boats, a cloud in the sky.

"You'd be able to know what they're thinking, those two, if you could find the four differences," Jeffrey prompted.

The defendants would grow agitated. Four! There were not four differences. There were buds on some of the trees and not others but this was the case in both pictures. In the land of the dead there were many cradles, sure. But why did they care what the man and the woman were thinking? It was no concern of theirs. They weren't even real as they themselves were real . . .

But to me he said, "Yours is an interesting case. I'll dispense with my usual queries."

"Do you remember when we first met?" I asked. "You had caught that little fish."

"On a bit of my nail. I had broken off a piece of my fingernail and put it on a hook," he said. "Let us not discuss the fish."

"The soul dwells in all things like a fish in the sea, like the sea in a fish," I suggested.

"That's no longer the case, I'm afraid," he said. "I'm going to give you a little something to read and then we'll talk about that instead. This is the story about the hunter Gracchus by Franz Kafka. When Gracchus falls off a precipice in pursuit of his prey, and bleeds to death and dies, he suffers the mishap of not actually dying. His death ship loses its way."

He handed me some pages and closed his eyes. I could sense how much he loved this room, his robes, the graceful carafe close to hand, the cactus in its little pot, the jury box unpeopled . . .

I read it carefully. I said, "There's much that seems unnecessary."

"Yes, it takes a while to get going, doesn't it. The hordes of children, the doves, the offal and the fruit skins lying about, the crowds dithering around the waterfront, the awkward floor plan of the yellowish two-storied house . . ."

"And is it not unnecessary that he is on both a great stair, an infinitely wide and spacious stair between two worlds, all the while he is on a ship, an ark, sailing on earthly waters to earthly ports?" I offered.

"A bark," Jeffrey said. "The vessel is a bark."

"A bark, rather."

"A bark needs winds, an ark not necessarily. What is a chamois?" he asked happily for he remembered with amusement that he knew a chamois as something his grandfather used on the days

he washed and waxed his great dark car, a proud and powerful machine so like his grandfather.

"A small goat-like antelope of Europe."

"You must forget such replies," he said. "I was only teasing."

"When Gracchus first awakens on his bier in the room where he's been taken, he forgets his situation," I said formally, unbothered by my student role. One should ever be a student of unfulfillable promise after all. "Then he remembers everything. The mishap, his constant wandering, the ports and towns, the official greeters and questioners, the indifference and incuriosity of everyone else. He remembers because he has not been dead always. Rather he is dead dead dead as he says, but in a certain sense, alive."

Jeffrey regarded his hands and nipped at one of the nails, a habit he could not break.

"An interesting case, isn't it?" he said. "Now let us read the fragment. I like fragments. Sometimes I prefer them to the whole."

He handed me further pages entitled "The Hunter Gracchus: A Fragment."

The copy was faint. I could barely make anything out. Briefly I saw the words "Leviathan world" but then I did not. The phrase had vanished. It was as though the page had momentarily desired to accommodate my need but then had withdrawn. I read more easily now but with less assurance.

"What do you think?" Jeffrey asked.

"Nothing further is revealed here," I replied. "The questioner is no longer an official greeter but a businessman who boards the ship out of curiosity. He seems most intent on informing Gracchus that no one thinks about him, that he is not a subject that is discussed."

"Is that true? Why would this be so?"

"Because thinking about him resolves nothing. Because life

is brief. It's as much as one can do just to get oneself through it. That's one of the explanations provided, anyway."

"What does the questioner, this curiosity-seeker, want here, anyway?"

"Coherence. A coherent story."

"And Gracchus mocks him for that, doesn't he. What does Gracchus want?" He took the pages from me and placed them on a shelf.

"To no longer have to endlessly question his situation. To no longer be an exception."

"What are the differences?"

"Between coherence and exception?"

"Between you and Gracchus."

"Gracchus is an invention of the writer Kafka."

"Perhaps not a pure invention," Jeffrey said. "Perhaps he adapted it from an old story, an old folk tale."

I felt the story was revelatory while being impossible to interpret. "Gracchus's death is incomplete," I offered. "In my situation it is my birth."

"No, no," he said. "I see that you were born and quite without difficulty. Something did happen after forty days, it's true, but you weren't gone long enough to make any real difference. Maybe you're a little more sensitive to loss. A bit more . . . incompatible. Are you suggesting that birth did not prepare you for life? How long did you stay in that place?"

"Until they left. They all left. Do you know what became of them?"

"What became of them?" he repeated, astonished. He shuddered remembering that place, so without form or spiritual industry. "Is this all you remember of your death?"

"I don't remember my death."

"You were a non-experiencer then possibly, which is just a psychological defense mechanism of depersonalization." He

grimaced. "Sometimes this loathsome cant just grabs me by the throat and tries to throttle . . ." He put on an aloof expression.

"I would like to take up living rather than remembering," I said. "I would like to take up the art of living for the first time."

"The art of living? You mean the work of living. No one takes up such labors for the first time."

But, he assured me, should he find in my favor, matters would be very different. The recipe would be changed. Not that he slavishly followed the recipe—he was no cookbook judge ever mixing the stale ingredients of precedent, principle and policy. He could interpret, over-apply when he so fancied. He could apply via the Mischief Rule. The Mischief Rule was a kick.

He dismissed me abruptly then. He told me to come back tomorrow.

I turned and was surprised to see that the courtroom was full of people, and the gallery as well. Had they been there all the while I was laboring over the hunter Gracchus? I blushed and hurried out. The door to the structure was narrowly tall and red. It was two doors actually, which met in a thin crease, so thin you could scarcely put a playing card between them.

I was not surprised that it was the child Jeffrey I had so soon encountered upon my emergence in the outside world. I had slipped into conversation with him as easily as Gracchus had into his winding sheet, *like a girl into her marriage dress*. I had not been discomfited because I believed I was still receiving instruction, but I now realized that further instruction might not be forthcoming.

Gracchus's story was without dignity or beauty, not that the author was obligated to traffic in such matters. It was artificial, preposterous, inconclusive, a game of meanings that could not be won. It demanded its opposite, the other story, its foil, its righteous adversary.

"Pilgrim!" a woman called to me from the shadows the building cast. "Pilgrim!" she called, amused.

"Are you to come back tomorrow as well?" I asked.

"No. He did not tell me to come back tomorrow."

"You're not his mother, are you?" I asked, recalling for an instant the old brusque bored glamor of Barbara.

"He's convinced our paths have never crossed before. 'Hath the earth a mother?' he asked me. 'Why do you want to cause so much trouble?' I said. 'Hath the rain a father?' he said, cool as can be."

Away from the square and the immense tree dripping dark was the brilliant shadeless shameless day. On the wide congested boulevard, a long car, a hearse, inched past.

"That thing always seems to be passing by," Barbara said. She pointed to a wad of pink chewing gum glistening on the fender. "And isn't that so humorous with those people inside, taking everything so seriously and not knowing it's there."

The car with its lustrously rude medallion flowed imperiously past, many of the vehicles in its wake pulling boats wobbling on trailers' worn wheels. The boats were beyond repair, warped and splintered, the strakes gaping, the shrunken seams uncaulked. Of beautiful design, now shorn of purpose, illegitimate. In Kafka's story, the boat, the *bark*, originally belonged to no one but then it had masters, who were Gracchus's masters, too, yet they died, they were ever dying, their last thoughts of Gracchus.

Behind the hearse, the mass moved forward, a paste of humans and machines, a retinue of the impatient—cursing the fates that had stuck them behind this horrid thing again.

"What!" Nolo cried. "Who!"

He had just nosed into the wildlife tunnel under the highway to take a piss. There weren't supposed to be any pedestrians down here, to say nothing of wildlife. It was for official use only.

But he'd detected something. Maybe it was some nature of non-human animal that could understand a directive and was trusting and therefore totally fucked.

The tunnel had been part of an old mitigation effort. *Mitigation.* No one knew the meaning of the word now. Words died like everything else.

He rolled down the window. There was just the sound of the truck's serpentine belt, loose again. He cut the engine. "Hey!" he called. When he was a kid, his mother would always correct him: *Hay is for horses . . .* her attempt at elevating him in the social niceties. His ma. The only one who knew he was incapable of doing what they had suspected him of doing. The only one! And they said: *It's because she's his ma and she's not that bright either . . .* She knew he was blameless, and so he was found to be. But no one apologized to him. No one said: *Sorry man, forgive us man, for thinking you did the unspeakable . . .* No one.

The tunnel stank of trapped diesel fumes and was beginning to leak. After it exited under the highway it ran under the lake. The paintings of the animals had long ago blistered and faded in the dampness. A bunch of autistic ladies in hats had done them. You had to be certifiably autistic to get any of the public artwork jobs in those days. It had been a flaky idea to paint animals on the walls as though it were a child's nursery. What was the link between animals and babies anyway? It was just a marketing convention. It was obvious as soon as a kid was old enough to throw a rock that there was no pact between them. After that the deal was pretty much: I get to kill you and you get to be dead.

Now anyone could create art as long as it was for consumption in public spaces. But it all had to be of the harrow. Goddamn harrow was everywhere.

He started the truck again and fishtailed away. Nothing was going to answer him down here. The tunnel weirded him out.

When he returned to Denver Erie Ford's the television was still on but the hockey game had been replaced by a film of babies crawling around a room.

"What are you doing?" Nolo asked.

"I'm trying to avoid the channel that just shows minutes of silence. They describe what the minute of silence is for and then they broadcast it. It's all some people watch. You know Crispy in billing?"

"No."

"It's all Crispy watches. Crew goes all over the world capturing solemn minutes of silence. Sometimes they lighten things up by showing people placing flowers and cards and teddy bears at some location, or another. You know from whence the idea of the teddy bear originated? It was in Colorado, my place of origin. Teddy Roosevelt was on a bear hunt and was unsuccessful. His friends presented him with a freshly dead cub to comfort him, in commiseration like. Tiny little thing. Cuddly. The idea caught on, with certain alterations. So what's going on out there, First Responder?"

"That is a shitload of babies," Nolo said, staring at the screen. "Where are they anyway? What are they doing?"

"It's some investigative projection into society's future needs, I think."

"I was a babysitter once."

"That I cannot believe."

"I was screwing the mommy."

"You devil."

"The baby had such a large head. There might have been something wrong with her from the start, actually."

"No, no, babies have big heads and I've got a theory as to why. Our relatively small heads have to do with civilization. Civilization provides us with buffers and protections separating us from

the natural world. Once, you were connected to the world and had to have continual awareness. Your brains had to be bigger and more receptive and your head had to be bigger to hold the brains. You had to know everything about your environment and now you don't. Babies are a throwback. Their heads get smaller soon enough."

"I gotta wash up," Nolo said. "You don't still urinate in the sink, do you?"

When he returned, Denver was saying, "I've fathered six kids all by different ladies and the remarkable thing is each mother considers theirs an indigo child. The women don't even speak to one another but they all came up with this loony indigo theory. The kids are all ADHD, disruptive and destructive and narcissistic as hell, but each mom, bless her heart, thinks her kid is a leap in human evolution, a shift in vibrational energy, a harbinger of changing consciousness. The kids just have serious psychiatric disorders if you ask me, too much Chardonnay in the womb."

"A tragedy," Nolo said, shrugging.

"The Tragedians asked Plato to let them put on some tragedies. Plato said, 'Very interesting, gentlemen . . .'"

"He did not say that."

"'. . . very interesting gentlemen, but I must tell you something. We have prepared here the greatest tragedy of all. It is called the State.'"

"I love the State."

"I know. You depress me. Anesthetizing state run by amoral functionaries. Tell me about the call you answered."

"Two old malcontents trying to blow up a facility. Fire's still burning. Nonetheless, damage was slight."

"Where do they come from? They keep coming."

"The babies?" He looked at the television where the babies

were bumbling about, like trout in a hatchery. No commentary was involved, or the sound was off. The set was immense and old-fashioned, a layer of visible dust clinging to the screen. How long had it been since Denver was given a leave of absence anyway?

"No, the grannies and pappies in their senile delinquent crusade."

"There are fewer of them all the time."

"You'd think they wouldn't bother. Did I ever tell you my pop's deathbed advice?"

"Yes."

"No I didn't. I'll tell you what it was. 'Try to get yourself killed.' His last words. He died after an extremely long illness. He lingered and lingered."

"What did he die of?"

"Environmental issues."

"I like that he said it but you lie, I think."

"But my pop was a loner. These old people are like a cult. Fanatic believers in the unsustainability of sustainability. How do they communicate with one another do you think? Gastric thumpings? Coded whistles at the knee replacement clinics? Pigeons?"

"Pigeons!"

"Homing pigeons, ice pigeons, passenger pigeons, Whoops no. Not passenger pigeons . . ."

He squinted at the television. "I swear that's one of my kids there. See the one punching the other one?"

They were silent for a while, watching the babies. Occasionally, another one was introduced into the mix, or so it seemed.

"Is one of those really yours?" Nolo asked.

"Look at the lighting fixtures, man, look at the smocks. This thing was filmed fifty, sixty years ago, and God knows where. Look, if I told you that if you were going to stay much longer I'd pass out and not wake up because in your absence I ingested a

number of pills as well as a considerable amount of alcohol, what would you say."

"Say?"

"Say, do, whatever," Denver said irritably.

"Well are you shitting me again like with the kid?"

Denver burped. Then he frowned.

"I'd say you were shitting me again like with the kid, that kid being your kid. You're discouraged because of your work. That work doesn't suit you. Nothing to be ashamed of. You got sick of people requiring assistance. Who wouldn't. The goal is to become transhumanized. The times demand it. This is something those people who require assistance will never understand. You have any pineapple? I could make us some pineapple spears."

"Look in the refrigerator," Denver said, closing his eyes. "Maybe Santa brought some."

There was nothing in the refrigerator save for a few badly misinformed flies. He had a keen longing for pineapple. It was a fabulous detoxifier as well as good for the skin and hair. Just because he never looked at himself didn't mean he was insensitive to appearance. He returned to the living room where Denver remained in his rat-colored La-Z-Boy staring glassily at his television.

Nolo turned it off.

"Thank you," Denver said. His face shone with sweat. "You know I couldn't get up right now if you paid me."

"Why would I pay you?"

The room in its silence sounded funny, like the woods— whatever was left of the skinny junked-up woods through which he sometimes ran—as though it were conscious, as though it was troubled. Then he heard sirens going off somewhere, then traffic and the sound of the refrigerator turning over, *turning over,* which is how his mother would put it as: *that refrigerator turns over too much, it's always waking me up . . .*

He pulled the phone from his pocket but then put it back. He picked up Denver's phone instead.

"What is the nature of your emergency?" a man's voice inquired.

"Denver's not well."

"Is this an individual or is it the bustling metropolis of several million cradled in the foothills of the Rocky Mountains and weaned on gold and silver wealth that once flowed from nearby mines?"

He was silent.

"Sorry," the dispatcher said. "We get a lot of crank calls. So this Denver is a person?"

"He's your predecessor. He's the guy who answered the phones before you."

"Where you calling from?"

"We're catercornered from you. We have a partially obstructed view of the Emergency Room awning."

"Catercornered?"

"Kitty-cornered."

"Oh, kitty-cornered."

"We're very close. It should take you a minute max to get over here. He's barely breathing."

"Is he breathing?"

"Yes."

"Is his situation the result of any weapon? Guns? Knives?"

"No."

"Is anyone at this address armed? Would anyone at this address pose a threat to rescue personnel?"

"Unlikely."

"And who is this? With whom am I speaking?"

He turned the phone off and left, propping the door open with one of Denver's shoes. He had enjoyed shooting the breeze with him. And he hoped Denver would get through this and accom-

plish his stated intention of metaphysical progress which personally Nolo did not believe in, though he could respect Denver's delusions about it. Everything was delusionary anyway, fleeting forms, empty fancies. Everything obliterated to make room for something else—that was the way of the world. This being the case, it always puzzled him that people expected so much from life.

He stopped at a supermarket, nodding at the armed guards in brotherly regard, and bought two outrageously priced pineapples. They were perfectly ripe. The stifling of their maturation had been calculated to the very moment they hit the shelves. He would eat both of them when he got back to his mother's house. Home. He shouldn't be living there still, he knew, he should get a tent, wickiup somewhere extremely noxious where he could be alone. He should burn the place down and walk away. He knew a girl once—it was right after the incident with the baby—who burned her house down after her mother died. One minute they were half-heartedly arguing about whose turn it was to change the kitty litter and the next minute the woman fell prey to a busting aneurysm. On the first month's anniversary, the house went down. The girl hadn't even let the cats get away, her mother's cats. Everything had to go, everything went. It was a gesture of devotion.

*My clothes and makeup, my Cuban heels,* the girl had said, *every pricey piece of electronic shit you can imagine. I had nice stuff but then I realized the impermanence of all things. It was as though someone poured ice water on my head. The revelation was that shocking.*

This discovery moved her deeply.

*No one wants to know the ramifications of this,* she said. *I know and I'm branded a freak. You're a freak, too, for different reasons of course.*

He protested this. He was not a freak. He was merely a dupe of fate implicated in a foul rumor. Nothing had happened to that child, that infant, but the mother had acted as though he'd sent the whole world over the edge. She'd gone nuts, like, that very night.

And it had certainly changed his life. He'd never had another woman, for one thing. He'd become a scapegoat, cast into the wilderness.

His own mother believed in God's mysterious ways all the more avidly. *You're the misunderstood innocent,* she assured him. *The fact you are blameless is all to the good, God's good. He's calling you, PeterPaul, calling you to a life of atonement, of reconciliation and reparation.*

He thought not, and said nothing.

The girl thought it obvious that they should be together, two outcasts scaling the watchtowers, skelter-helter, throwing away their lives at every opportunity.

But her father installed her in a clinic from which no juvenile had escaped in all its many years of covert and controversial operation, remarried, and moved away. PeterPaul, now utterly friendless, was expected to move away as well but he did not. He and his mother stayed on, objects of avoidance and distrust. His mother grew flakier by the day, saying her rosary, smoking her weed, dreaming of the poppy-red Mercedes that would run on old cooking oil.

*I want to tell you something, son. I've been fibbing you. I don't like God all that much. That little baby He had you watching and then Him visiting her in that weird way He did and putting you in that awful position. It colored your whole life.*

But maybe that was God's plan for me, Ma, to give me a darkly colored life.

He did not say this in earnest.

*He don't have a plan for any of us, PeterPaul. He just uses us or not, willy-nilly. But we won't show the white feather, will we.*

We don't have the white feather, Ma. We've never had it.

*We get along good, don't we, son.*

They got along good and then she was gone.

He emptied his pockets on a table of scratched plastic.

There was the old dead guy's little scroll, a pack of gum, his own truck keys. He thought of the countless awful meals he and his ma had shared at this table, the mumbled prayers, the soiled napkins, all the while something was passing, happening, unobserved. He picked up the keys. He would drive back to Denver's. He would access the minutes-of-silence channel with him. He missed Denver. He should have done more. Instead he had tossed him away like a used match.

Jeffrey was in his chambers, dipping a cookie into a glass of milk.

*It doesn't make sense* he said soundlessly and widened his eyes.

*It's not fair* he mimed and pouted.

The milk wasn't satisfactorily cold. It wasn't easy to keep milk cold once you started to drink it. It was well nigh impossible.

*I don't understand why I'm here* he whined soundlessly in imitation.

Usually he wasn't this mean. He did not mock or presume. He did not take his position for granted. He was dignified and appreciative. He loved his work, the law. He was born for the bench. Because of his seniority and at his request, he didn't get the drunks. The drunks gave him hives, and they made him very, very impatient. He'd take a mass murderer or technological utopian over a drunk any day.

But in general those who came before him were all pretty much the same. He kept in mind the note Darwin had scribbled to himself when he was hashing out evolution. "Never use the words *higher* and *lower*." He'd buy that note if he could. Get a nice frame for it. Maybe it would come up for auction. Stuff always did. There'd always be collectors, always vaults. Better to store seeds than scribblings in his informed opinion, however.

He put the cookie and milk aside. Best part of his day, cloying aftertaste and all. He'd wearied of the frightened surprise the

majority exhibited in the courtroom when they perceived him, a mere child.

At the age of ten, neurological development is pretty much complete, he'd sometimes take the bother of telling them. You knew that, did you not?

They did not.

There were things he'd like to do, sure. He'd like to change his name. He'd like to be called . . . Enoch. From henceforth, Enoch . . . who was taken from earth by the Almighty without passing through death.

You'd think more would have been made of such an accomplishment.

He'd like to play in the snow. He'd like to make a snowman. But there was no snow.

He'd like to shout *Clear the courtroom!*

He'd always wanted to do that, though it would be frightfully irresponsible.

Yet he'd had that interesting case this morning. Her visit was not totally unexpected. *You,* he thought. *All but born you.*

He ruffled himself in his black robes much as a bird would in her feathers.

Clear the courtroom, he said without speaking. Playfully.

Jeffrey—*Enoch*—went to the windows and looked down toward the park. There was the interesting case. Quite alone. As an interesting case she could anticipate no present moment, she possessed only the future, which she was still powerless to change.

He studied her a while longer and the shrunken space before which she fretted. Even in his time it had been larger, a whatya-callit, a sacred grove, a *temenos.* It had once meant asylum and within it one was *asulos*—the inviolable. It protected what was within and excluded that which was without. You can't beat Greek, he thought. He felt a special relationship with the great Hellenes. They had invented logic, had they not? *Temenos.* The word comes

from *temno*, to cut. Something cut from the meaningless, profane layer of life, something removed and isolated for a special purpose.

In fact it was the trees that had been cut cut cut, for there had been many more even in his time, a veritable grove of them. Now there was the one. And there were designs on that. He'd heard the rumors in his own courtroom. Once that tree came down, the place could be rechristened as a soccer field. First thing to be established after a catastrophe, or after a war peters out. Shows it's OK to have fun again—shows the indomitability of the human spirit. Outside the park the earth was spongy, flooded, soft. It was practically smoking—a not fit dwelling place. How small the enclosure had become.

He glanced at the sky. Disheartening. The Greeks were blind to blue and green. They would have perceived this sky to be in fact what it was—an excrementitious brown.

He had told her to come back. What a folly, perhaps even an injustice. It was unprecedented, but he was curious about her. And of course she dizzyingly brought back that peculiar interlude when he was adrift, dependent, when he didn't know what he was. Uncomfortable. Uncomfortable in his own skin. But he'd had the law even then, which he could mimic, and the law's blustering treaties with the dead.

He pictured the hunter Gracchus in his courtroom, fresh off the black bark—ice encrusting its rotting sails—carted in under a floral bedsheet. His presence would be no more unusual than what had happened that day with her showing up.

But he was confident that with a little ingenuity, he could resolve that case. Gracchus was just a simple man of the forest, at sea, a fish out of water, not up to the demands of his situation. He'd issue a few writs, tour the vessel perhaps, find the wormhole. Kafka need not be involved.

Gracchus, the literal expression in a concrete image of an abstraction. That was what Kafka did best. And what a comedian!

The peculiar painting in the ship's cabin. The doves. The fifty little boys in attendance. Gracchus's dog . . .

Had there been dogs?

He frowned. He'd been told he had a mind like a steel trap. He *did* have a mind like a steel trap. But did Gracchus have dogs when he fell down that ravine? He returned to his desk and picked up the same pages he had given her to read. He read them carefully. There was the wind, the wine, the doltish inquiries. Always the wrong questions! There were the fifty little boys. But the dogs had vanished from the story for some reason.

Jeffrey suddenly felt a great weariness. He rubbed his eyes. His grandfather had told him that if he rubbed his eyes, religiously as it were, he'd make them larger and thus be more commanding in court.

The diameter of the human eye is about 10 percent of the height of the head, his grandfather said. If you could boost your eye index up to say 18 percent . . . 20 percent would be superb, you'd have them quaking in their undies.

*Dad, Dad*, his father would say, *you're scaring him.*

*I am not scaring this boy*, his grandfather would say.

*You're scaring me, Dad.*

*That's because you are not him*, his grandfather would say. *You're a burbling disappointment, a little teapot.*

*Jeffrey*, his grandfather would address him once more: *Glaukopis. Owl-eyed, the great Athena's epithet. Wisdom, Jeffrey, knowledge. Let the great owl-eyed Athena be your guide.*

And Jeffrey would rub his eyes until they burned.

Ahh, what was the point . . . Sure he was commanding in court, sure he had them quaking in their undies, but what were wisdom and knowledge these days? Knowledge had deteriorated into mere detection and diagnosis. And you could train a giant pouched African rat for that. In three weeks a giant pouched rat from that

once intriguing continent could be taught to sniff out land mines as well as most drugs and weapons. They could detect cancer in the unsuspecting, too, but their trainers didn't want to burn them out with the boredom that too much success brings. In any case, everyone had cancer these days . . . cancer, Parkinson's, leukemia, tumors, the sugar. Even a rat needs a challenge.

Owlet Jeffrey—*Enoch*—longed for the pickup another cookie would bring but he was an owlet of habit and structure. There would be no second cookie. He gave his eyes one more nostalgic swipe, left his chambers and descended to the courtroom to confront all those who had fallen under his jurisdiction.

It's a serious matter to allow someone to wander among the living after their death. Or before they were born. Or, as she had argued, before their birth was fully accomplished. Is that what she'd said? Yes. And he had said that many feel that way about themselves without being actually aware of it. By which he meant that they become human without knowing the first thing about it, the requirements and such. That is, they suspected they were meant to be more or different but fumbled about in the smoky light of half-realized lives instead. That is . . .

He never should have sent her away. What if something befell her and she didn't come back? Maybe he should go out and get her. But that would be unprecedented too. That would be the eighth day all right, the one that St. Augustine refers to, after the seven days of creation, the one with no evening to it.

"Your Honor," some supplicant was murmuring, "I accept the unethical acts of my past. I tell you this sincerely and I wish therefore to alter their meaning."

"Excuse me?" Enoch said. "Alter their meaning? That's a good one. What's your name?"

"Castor."

"As in Castor and Pollux? Where's your brother?"

"I don't know no Pollux. I'm not responsible for no Pollux but I accept the unethical acts of my past and wish to be allowed to alter their meaning."

"You don't want forgiveness then?"

"I don't believe there's any benefit to that. Is there?"

"What's it feel like accepting your past?"

"I feel like a new man."

"That's the dumbest thing I've heard yet," Enoch said. "Go over there, no there, to the left. Lie down over there. This court is in perpetual session."

A woman was next, looking close to fainting.

"Don't be frightened," he said in what he hoped was not too unctuous a fashion.

"I planted butterfly bushes once but they, the butterflies, didn't come."

"Yes, well, I've heard that employees in these mega gardening centers don't know what they're talking about."

"I even thought of suing them, not the butterflies of course."

She faded away and was replaced by a man who said in a loud aggrieved voice, "I wanna work with survivors, I wanna dig survivors out of the rubble and build privies and shelters. Fuck the earth. The earth is worthless . . . Long live the earth who has freed us from the obligation to save her! You're not gonna catch me serving the earth as if she were some sort of goddess, I want to serve my own kind."

"Remove him at once," Enoch said. As an afterthought he said, "Give him some privies to build."

"I guess I'm next, am I next?" a young woman asked. "OK then, my mother kept rabbits. She collected them. It was so embarrassing. People called her the Bunny Lady. Otherwise she was normal. We had a little shed in the yard which should have been my playhouse but it was always full of rabbits. After I went to Yale she was arrested for having so many rabbits and I had to post bond.

She was told not to go within one hundred yards of a rabbit. But she violated her probation and I was asked to post bond again but I didn't, I didn't post bond."

"Now you want to know if you should have laughed or cried," Enoch said.

"That's right. I didn't know whether to laugh or cry at the time."

"What did you do?"

"Neither. I went out and bought shoes."

"Then that was the wrong response I guess," Enoch said. "Is your mother still alive?"

"Dead and buried now. They won't have to worry that she'll get within one hundred yards of a rabbit anymore."

"Umm," Enoch said. "Have you heard the old belief that when you shiver for no reason it's because a rabbit is running over your grave?"

The woman laughed in a projectile fashion before being led away.

So it went. Hundreds in an hour under his purview.

And the things they tried to sneak past him! One old soul had arrived clutching her bottle of vinegar, the old-fashioned kind with that cobwebby stuff floating around in the bottom of it. They brought sandwiches, pills, an *alebrije* with a broken tail. Some had pieces of plastic that once had given them anything they wanted that they still clutched like amulets. Some were surprisingly argumentative given the circumstances.

One fellow strode before the bench and announced, "You ain't God."

Enoch sighed. "I am not," he said. "Look at these pictures. Do you see the diff . . ."

"Because I believe in God and the God I believe in will bring me back like I've always been, same way of doing things, same way of figuring . . ."

"The same apprehensions," Enoch said, preferring formal usage.

"I'm not apprehensive about nothing because God will bring me back and it will be me, not just someone like me, but I won't need to be concerned about what I've done or worry I should have done something different."

"You regret nothing?"

"Wouldn't question God, Shortstack."

Jeffrey regarded him sourly. "Did anyone in your family cut that tunnel through Wawona?"

"Through what?"

"Wawona, the giant sequoia."

"Oh, yeah. That tree older than Jesus that you could drive your car through for fun? One of my father's brothers did that. Real outdoorsy type, was able to sign on as part of the crew. My mother had a photograph of him and it was in the kitchen for a while. Nobody ever called it 'Wawona' though."

He looked somewhat stupefied, then bored, then impatient. Then he grabbed his chest and said something that sounded very much like "ghh."

"Oh my," Jeffrey said.

"I think I'm having a heart attack. Owww, it hurts like a motherfucker. Owww." He sank to the floor and disappeared.

Jeffrey rose and peered over the great walled desk but could see no sign of him. He had simply disappeared. Jeffrey hadn't even given a ruling, though it certainly would have been dismissal with extreme prejudice. It would have been well-nigh impossible for the ruling to be arbitrary, capricious, contrary to law, an abuse of discretion and not supported by objective evidence in this case. Maybe in the more obvious ones he should pick up the pace a bit. He hoped he wasn't losing focus. He felt at times almost bodiless, just a massive ten-year-old brain presiding. Or a blossom, tossed about by the wind. The wind. How the wind had howled in that

asylum by that aphotic lake! It was ceaseless. No wonder they'd all been nuts. You'd think his mother would have been more careful about their itinerary. He was the product of erratic parenting . . . When he was six she'd told him that when her time came, as she phrased it, she wanted to be cremated and her ashes stored in a martini shaker. He had said that he found the request exceedingly frivolous and he would never honor it. She had accused him of having no sense of style but the matter had not come up again.

His mother. He hadn't thought of her in what seemed centuries. It was a peculiar day. He raised his arms, making the robes crepitate in that way that he liked, and thought again of that cloudland on the lake where elders and radical sickies prepared, prepared . . . He didn't know exactly how they'd gotten there but he imagined the strange resolve descending upon them—like a cloud, was the best he could ever come up with for he did not have much of an imagination, he'd be the first to admit, a fact he wasn't about to lose any sleep over, he who never slept. Maybe they saw Death studying them in that weary heavy-lidded way Death affected and they realized they didn't want to donate their organs or give their last nickel to that holier-than-thou kid tricycling for charity. They felt bad and they would never feel good again. Bad and mad. They didn't want to be reliable anymore or well-adjusted or accommodating or moderate or accepting.

And then the cloud, which was not a cloud in the literal atmospheric sense—*cloud*, after all, arising from the Greek *gloutos*, buttock for heaven's sake—indicated to them something along the lines of *What do you have to lose?* for society was still counting on them, heavily, to think they had something still to lose.

He sympathized with the old delinquents actually. And then she showed up and asked what had become of them. It was depressing.

He was still peering into the space into which the disputatious fellow had vanished. Had he really called him . . . Shortstack . . . ? That was perturbing. He raised his eyes and regarded his court-

room. The procedural unintelligibility of it all! Well, he'd wanted this. He'd wanted it very much.

He called for a recess and retreated to his chambers. The cases would be piling up, he was well aware. Men and women—even children, for he'd noticed one playing with a little truck, rolling it back and forth—would be creeping up the stairs in fetid flood if he continued to take these breaks. They'd smother him if they detected the slightest whiff of uncertainty or avoidance on his part. They'd roll right over him. Humanity could be quite overwhelming.

Who was he kidding. Humanity *was* overwhelming.

Goodness, how he would like to leave and seek her. He would pass through the court like a williwaw, leaving petitioners flailing to remain upright, their garments bloating out as though harboring the drowned. Someone would say, *"In deep space there's winds that blow a million miles an hour and this was like that."* And someone else would be sure to contest it. *"A wind like that's unmeasurable, someone's pulling your leg."* There wasn't much he couldn't predict his court rats saying, querulous and opinionated as they were to the end.

She'd been right here before him and he had dismissed her. He had invited her back, yes, but would she be able to return? He couldn't leave to go to her. His own masters wouldn't let him. And they'd been good to him, kept him as a kid, allowed him all the bells and whistles, the robes and polished rails, allowed him ultimate authority over all who had lived so carelessly and onerously on the earth with such savagely entitled abandon, and even those who hadn't. They had allowed him his incommutable sentences. The only thing they hadn't allowed was the bringing back of his tata, his grandfather whose murder at the hands of his simpleminded devil of a father Jeffrey still had difficulty comprehending. The murder of the father, heinous, heinous. Only murder of the mother being more so, a collective action proceeding pretty

much without cease if you addressed it in the lyrical entirety of *mother planet.*

Oh he couldn't wait until she returned.

*Don't wait then,* his grandfather would tease when Jeffrey would squeak his enthusiasm for some promised upcoming outing—a trial lawyer's convention, tea with a retired federal judge, a visit to juvenile court (the juvies frightened him somewhat actually). *Then don't wait,* his grandfather would say solemnly, *do anything but wait.*

And Jeffrey would never fail to find this amusing. His grandfather was known for his dry-as-a-desert wit. How he loved him. Ashes now. No more than the ashes of a book that had been poked about in a fire to provide a moment's warmth.

He did not understand how he could have gone on living after his grandfather died, after he *knew* his grandfather had died, for there had been seven days when he had not known and when he had missed him as one merely misses the temporary absence of a living loved one. There were no phones in the queer place where his mother had deposited them for a "holiday." That was the explanation she had given for the disturbing silence from home. When he'd whined and inquired further, his mother told him that Thomas Edison had failed in his attempt to build a phone that he anticipated would bear messages back and forth across the veil, and if Thomas Edison had failed, wasting years of his life and becoming half-dotty by the quest, it was unlikely that such an apparatus could be found even where they were. Jeffrey hadn't known what she was talking about. His grandfather had never spoken of Thomas Edison, thus he could not be of the Bar and was of little consequence. His mother's pronouncements had become more and more irregular and incomplete due to her drinking.

Seven days and not a sign. Though he tortured himself frequently with the thought that his grandfather *had* appeared

to him during that time on the shore of that disorienting lake, that he had in fact appeared as the small and helpless fish he'd caught.

Jeffrey took a deep and shaky breath. He had hyperventilated before when considering this. He had almost lost it actually when that very person, the interesting case, had brought up the soul like the fish in the sea, like the sea in the fish business.

He shoved his hands in his mouth and chewed. Oh that dreadful lake, that awful place with its drifting shades. How had his mother even come across it? It must have been by accident but she behaved as though it had been their destination all the while. We want your nicest room, she'd demanded at the desk, but of course there were no nicest rooms. Outside was even worse. There was a warped ping-pong table lacking a net, a structure with baffling signage toward which the other guests had streamed with disturbing ceremony and a not very clean swimming pool. What if he had wanted swimming lessons? What if he had wanted his mother to place her hand beneath his fragile spine and support him in clean cool waters? Beneath his vulnerable body would be a hand and the palm of this hand would be the point of secure serene balance upon which he would float . . . What if he had wanted that! He did not know how to swim to this day. And nobody seemed to eat there. The place certainly took away his appetite although in the beginning he'd missed his morning wheat germ. His mother had packed no bags for them. He didn't even have his *Black's Law Dictionary* or his dental floss. And then they left, as abruptly as they had arrived, and it was that night that his mother, in the bubble of their speeding car, had told him that his tata, his only advocate and ally, was dead.

He had been sing-songing to himself, having recently discovered the struggling field of animal law. "Animal use law prohibits any necropsy or surgical procedure on an animal within the sight

of other animals of the same species," he warbled, which was interesting, really interesting in that it acknowledged the distress and empathy of animals over . . .

"What?" he said.

"I believe the disagreement between your father and your grandfather was over procedural rather than substantive matters," she said, making every effort to present it in a way he'd appreciate.

When he said nothing, she said, "Your father will probably get off on the self-defense gambit, for your grandfather did brandish a stone paperweight at him."

"Which stone paperweight," Jeffrey said.

"What a funny question. It's practically inappropriate."

"He has many stone paperweights." Any rock can become metamorphic, his tata had told him.

"Well perhaps he had."

"Take it back what you said."

"Don't be difficult, Jeffrey. There's nothing Mother can do about it. Now you know what's what and we have to get back to what's what."

He was silent.

"Jeffrey," his mother said, "don't play with your thoughts."

He had seized the wheel then. His mother screamed and, struggling with him, quite naturally lost control of the vehicle which rolled and rolled as though it were a perfect orb designed to roll forever before it cast him out to stand alone on a dark road . . .

Jeffrey's head was pounding. He must be dehydrated. He poured water from the carafe into a shallow cup and studied it for a moment before gulping it down. The Greeks had their *psychomanteums* which were oracles of the dead appearing as visions in pools or certain pans of water. He'd never been granted such a vision, not as much as a peek. He had to be content with the constant revelation that most of what passed as the substance of

life was nothing. Still, he found the *psychomanteum* a somewhat attractive notion. Maybe he wasn't giving it enough time.

For a while as a child he had harbored the notion that when someone you were fond of died, it was yourself who disappeared. It began with his grandmother. She must have been baffled when everyone and everything she'd surrounded herself with vanished—her brilliant husband, her frivolous son and his awful wife—right down to her wispy grandson, her pet koi and the wedding ring she was always taking off and misplacing when she washed the dishes.

It was yourself who disappeared, the one who was supposed to be left, and you were never that person again.

He could hear the crowd below him multiplying. Really, he was falling further and further behind. Sometimes he tried to perceive them all as sacred clowns—holding nothing sacred, they point the way to the sacred.

But he could not do this often. Practically never.

The sound was quite extraordinary.

He remembered the description in an old book of a phenomenon long since vanished from the world, the sound of birds, of migrating wings passing through the darkness *in countless armies with a velvety rustle long drawn out.*

This was not that.

It was a rumbling metallic demanding cacophony, murderously sociable, pathologically multiplying.

He rushed down to them in a rage and did a week's work in an hour before retreating once more to his chambers, feeling a bit off his game. His tata always allowed his opponent to state his whole case, making sure the other had nothing more to say before the implacable rejoinder came. His tata was a man made of dynamite! He spoke and suddenly everything was inverted, all previous certainties were made questionable, everything reasonably argued

preposterous. His irrefutable triumph was thrilling to observe, a magic show, a pure confoundment . . .

He allowed himself a moment of wild adoration for the old man, then several more resigning his father to ever deeper hells.

But Jeffrey was not his grandfather, alas, and the interesting case was not an opponent. His divine opposite, perhaps, his challenge and check. She saw the tears in things which he did not; he saw only the injustice. Every person under his purview considered themselves unique as snowflakes but in the aggregate they were a blizzard, a whiteout of swirling expectation and denial. Yet still the rumor in his courtroom was that if his opinion was favorable, one should have no fear, if unfavorable, no hope. Which was pretty darn flattering to overhear, praise practically.

The truth of the matter was his judgments scarcely varied.

Scarcely do we inhume the wreckage of our lives than we dig it up again. That is why we keep on and keep on and keep on, never progressing except in the grossest and most mundane fashion, he would sometimes confide.

And then she appears and says she wants to take up the work of living for the first time!

*Art* of living, she'd actually said, which he corrected. She was thinking without the right words. She should just go to the next step of thinking with no words at all. He was able to do this on occasion, though the moment always caught him unaware, and he found it wonderfully refreshing and instructive. That was no way to explain it of course.

His masters had brought them together, but were they her masters as well? If they were, he thought somewhat anxiously, they might be requiring more of her than of him. Sometimes he wondered if they were even following his labors anymore, if the minute distinctions he did make were of any concern to them.

What if she were the world's last night? Isn't that the great

theological question—what if this present were the world's last night? Or one of the great questions, anyway, those who cared had so many of them.

But the governing authority, of which his court was very much not a part, was taking increasing measures to eliminate night. Instinctively if not metaphysically, they sensed a final reckoning and determined, being sovereign and all, that they would not be out-reckoned. Unnatural light would suffuse the all as soon as natural light began to wane. That was the assurance and the goal. Night generated unhealthy thinking anyway. And they found that people had no trouble sleeping without darkness, they'd be sleeping anyway, in the most profound sense they were always sleeping.

Even she slept, he suspected. For she couldn't remember her death! Which had been given to her for a purpose, after all. She was a human child. She wasn't born in a buttercup. She had endured the brief and starving banality of one of those last childhoods before eluding the great attrition and corresponding exculpatory resolve of the survivors, before being cosseted by brooding over-the-hill eco-nuts whose concern for the tusked and shelled, the finned and winged, made them the shame of their species and more outcast than any Azazel goat of the Hebrews. And now she was here, the last of her kind, or the first—the difficulties being the same—having realized her situation only when she became alone, when her familiars had vanished with the vanquished world.

But what was the point of coming back from the dead if only to visit the dead . . .

He tidied the papers on his desk once more. There were no dogs in the Kafka story. He wondered what else he'd been wrong about.

He resumed staring into the dish of water. There was a small insect there, a spider imperceptibly translucent, floating not on

the water but seemingly on an invisible film above it. It puzzled him, for the sterility of his chambers he had never questioned. It puzzled him for he could not ever remember seeing a spider before, which surely was impossible.

The spider brings the web out of herself and then lives in it. Remarkable.

The youth flagged Nolo down. "Your grille's all smashed in, you hit something?" he asked eagerly.

"You want me to hit you?"

"There's someone loitering in the park, won't leave, won't talk. I think she's an enemy of humanity," he said somberly.

"Yeah? Why?"

"She had that look."

Nolo regarded him. He was a fool. They were making more and more fools. The factory never quit, the machine never broke down, just kept stamping and spitting them out. "That's extremely helpful," he said. "Anything else?"

"She looked like she was waiting on somebody, some time for it to be or something."

"You're being remarkably detailed in the most helpful way. Have you ever considered a career in enforcement?"

"Yeah!" the youth said. "You gonna make her leave? Can I come with you?"

"Actually," Nolo said, "she'd have to be hurt, injured in some way, at death's door, about to greet the pale summoner, to warrant my presence."

"You're not going to ask her to explain herself?"

"If I were to ask her anything, I'd say, 'Would you have wanted to change anything, dear?'"

"'Dear!'" he exclaimed. "I tried to talk to her but she didn't say jack to nothing. I tell you she was weird."

"If she's still there tomorrow I'll take a look."

"If you make her leave I bet she'd have no place to go. I was looking like I wasn't paying attention but I was observing her closely. She looked like she could only see the black side of our works, our institutions and convictions."

"*Our* works, institutions and convictions," Nolo said, amused. "You're a bold little brat, aren't you."

"I mean no disrespect of course. I just meant she looked homeless, uncomfortable, not on board. Like I mentioned, she didn't say nothing. She didn't have language like."

"When it's a matter of death, the dream speaks another language."

"I don't like substitutions. Everything in a dream is a substitution, right? It's your unconscious. I never dream but a couple nights ago I see this horse banging around in my apartment and he crashes through the door and into the hall and out the window and I see it all broken and smashed up on the street below. I live a couple stories up and I felt kind of sorry for it but it looked kind of stupid down there too."

"That is not a propitious dream," Nolo said admiringly.

"The unconscious life is not worth living in my opinion," the youth said. "I don't believe in the unconscious life."

"Really my friend, the prognosis for you is not good."

"The horse is me, you're saying."

"No, no, of course not," Nolo said, quite impressed by the boy's utter ignorance. He wanted to put him in a headlock and pound him pulpy. "It's worse than that even, it's what you could have been."

"Yeah," the youth scoffed. "Something crazy-frightened, unhinged, in the wrong environment."

Nolo felt irritable once more. He no longer wanted to pound him pulpy, he wanted to find him so disposed and kneel to piously administer his useless nostrums. Then just as suddenly he felt

kindly and grievously toward him, as toward his own child, one he'd commandeered from a pup.

"Look," he said, "you're interrupting me. I got a place I got to go."

"It's one emergency situation after another I bet. They're getting more and more stupendous, aren't they? I want to do triage. I want to specialize in it. That's what I'm angling for. You're not gonna catch me out on the smoking oceans checking drops of seawater for signs of life, I'm not the monitoring kind."

"No," Nolo said, fascinated. The air felt like soup that he was being forced to eat. His eyes stung as though he'd finally lost immunity to the toxins of life, his life, all the while this youth, this product, was talking easily, confidently on.

"Yeah, triage. I'm going to specialize in priorities, transitions. A horse dumb enough to suicide out of a fourth-floor window isn't going to be high on my list."

"No time for the beasts of the world, naturally," Nolo said.

"That's right. Neither the actual ones or the not-me's either. Isn't that what you said my dream meant?"

"Many have that dream," Nolo said.

The boy reddened. "I'm just saying the one in the park warrants your attention or harassment at least. People should pay to regard that tree if that's all they're doing. The crazy ones should pay."

"So that's what she's doing? Regarding the tree, nothing else? That tree's going to be removed tomorrow, you know."

"I thought it was soon! Any day I've been thinking for a while now, any day! It's a big old sucker."

"Yes it is."

"I thought there was going to be an announcement, so we could all partake of history."

"I'm the announcement. You've heard the announcement from me."

"It'll be the last of the shit that's come before," the youth said with some awe.

Nolo parked and made his way to Denver's door. The ground was noxious and damp, just as it always was. Bad for his boots. Inside there was nothing but the television, the walls around the squat appliance soiled from the drinks and food Denver had gotten into the habit of throwing in irritation at what he had chosen to watch. Denver's meals had been flagrantly unhealthy, Sonoran hot dogs, gravy fries, cheesy noodles. He was a devotee of two-for-one offers. This is going to expire *tomorrow,* he would say troubled, clutching some wrinkled coupon. But Denver had an ascetic streak as well and what he'd died of was disgust. Disgust assisted by drugs. Disgust abetted by too much reading of unfashionable tragedies and newly acquired Six Step ambitions.

First you seek, he told Nolo. You gotta want to seek. You can't cease the seeking. Then you find. But that's not enough, it doesn't stop there. After finding you have to suffer great disturbance, psychological disturbance. Some people can't get past this one. They're stuck, lost, they flip out. If you can withstand disturbance there comes amazement. This is very cool and transformative. Then comes total control of yourself and your perceptions. Then the final step, the culmination . . . rest.

Nolo thought it was a lot to go through just to reach rest, or *repose,* as Denver said sometimes. Repose sounded even worse.

But Nolo would grant that the Six Step required industrial-strength integrity and he'd never thought his friend had that much integrity. But sometimes it comes down to integrity vs. survival, does it not?

In any case, Denver had found his repose. He was gone and the chair he'd been sprawled in. His books were gone, too, those dirty paperback tragedies he'd so adored.

The big screen possessed a faint glow, waiting for the next tenancy. When his mother died he hadn't been in the room. He'd been at the hospital but on a different floor, having just brought in one of those tiresome oldsters who were trying to save the planet, last of the pelicans he thought of them as, trying to revive what they loved with their own blood. His mother was dead on a narrow bed and they'd left the heart monitor on beside her showing its green straight line and he'd thought it cruel. It was probably policy, it was most assuredly policy to provide this ultimate assurance of a change in station and he had seen it hundreds of times but it surprised him here next to his mother and it offended him and he thought it cruel.

Nolo sat cross-legged on the floor. It was not quiet here. The sounds of sirens, traffic, screams and laughter slipped through the walls though the walls were not thin, they were ugly cement blocks, the place was a sealed fortress in appearance only. The youth in the park had depressed him. Heartless little turd. The harrow had initially been perceived as brutally and blithely indiscriminate, but further studies indicated that those it spared were rigidly optimistic, uninhibited and chary of any devotion. Kid was a perfect specimen. The profile was holding up pretty well as people rushed to embrace those characteristics to prove their own legitimacy. Of course studies were always shifting, changing, coming up with some new angle, affirming the opposite of what they'd just assured everyone about. Now it was being discovered that some were prone to dying from the harrow's requirements after being initially spared. He believed that Denver was now of that number. He had become too sensitive, in his fashion, to continue if not necessarily thrive. Actually no one was expected to thrive.

The one that brat in the park had gotten so twisted up about, he was going to leave her alone. He wasn't going to investigate. What would he question her about anyway? People pass through.

That's all they do really. She was probably gone now, gone to the coast with all the streaming others, the sea, as though the sea hadn't already happened.

Nolo wanted to remain in this emptied room. He didn't want to go back. Stillness. Focus. Do not recollect. Do not desire. *You're the messenger,* Denver had said, and it wasn't the first time. He was always saying stuff like that. *Be the messenger.* And he was. This was what he was. But he wasn't the message.

The mayor had been having the most godawful dreams. Not dreams exactly, more like nightmares. Though not nightmares as much as a sensation that he was being torn limb from limb.

He didn't understand it. His job was not that stressful. It was an honorary position though he was allowed the courtesy of a few pronouncements. He'd once been—God it seemed a lifetime ago—a salesman. And a brilliant one, he could sell a shock collar to a Doberman, though he dealt in vehicles. He could spot a moral hazard a mile away and was expert at taking full advantage of the situation. Poor bastard would default on payments causing his credit rating which was no less than his very being to be ruined, initiating a cascade of torment by steroidal bounty hunters with Tasers and Flameless Expulsion Grenades in their butt-packs.

He'd gone on to refine his gift, selling partial zero-emission vehicles at high cost to those who purported to give a damn. *Stuff coming out of the pipe is cleaner than the air outside . . . You can suck on it as if you were in two places at once, that is, in the driver's seat and not in the driver's seat . . .*

That was long ago. He'd sold a lot of cars. There'd once been a rumor someone wanted to assassinate him for God's sake. But he'd made it through. And now he was addressed as mayor and life was about as gratifying as could be expected under the circumstances.

Though lately he'd had a most unpleasant vision that they were all living in an open grave and that any welcome order that had been reestablished depended rather overmuch on sweeping the sides, the many walls of the grave.

This notion had been difficult to quash and he'd only been moderately successful. Then came these horrid physical sensations when he was trying to nap. He felt he was being stretched on a rack, quartered like a lamb, thrown down and dragged by a galloping horse. He was left understandably exhausted. He needed a sabbatical though he worried what a sabbatical might mean at his age. Still, he could trim his schedule somewhat. There was no need to take down that goddamned tree right now just so a ribbon could be cut for another goddamned soccer field. He'd postpone the event.

Jeffrey's tata had read Kafka to him before bedtime as a special treat. The fellow's work was not unknown to him. He liked the story about the doctor and the boy, the boy whose gaping wound the doctor had not noticed on his first examination. That was a good one. He'd always rather—what do they say—*identified* with the boy, though he'd never been sick himself. He'd never even been to the dentist. He had remarkably good teeth. He could concur completely with everything Kafka wrote about the endless courts and trials, the innumerable hordes and refused petitions (that nevertheless being rejected granted the petitioner a kind of relief), even the very gruesomeness of the living present that Kafka so fancied. But, as he had reflected previously, Kafka could do only so much. Gracchus had been given his wearying sentence because of his guilt. He had roamed the fruitful earth and had taken from it in a contented stupor and when he died his death was as incomplete as his life had been.

Jeffrey felt indisposed, grumpy. He went to the window and

looked down at the square. She was not there. Had that place once
been a cemetery? *Cemetery*—from the Greek *koimeterion*, sleep-
ing chamber, akin to the Latin, *cunae*, cradle.

Things used to add up, not so much anymore.

When she returned, he, Enoch—Enoch! He had to get into the
habit—would ask her to write something, a fragment. *The Hunter
Gracchus: Fragment Two.* She could do whatever she wanted within
the general outline. She could have the mayor say something intel-
ligent for a change, put in dogs, alter the picture in the cabin, even
give Gracchus a companion who ever accompanied him. Why
not? Kafka's story was so heavy, so masculine. Gracchus was so
crude, so filled with thoughtless violent happiness as he lay in
ambush, as he slayed the innocent. Everything was masculine,
stubborn, ponderous, heavy, even the wine was heavy.

His companion's name could be Galena.

Even better, Galena would become Gracchus. There would be
no Gracchus. The green Galena, the name of a promising stone
in alchemical circles. The green Galena . . .

How would she be received, this initiator, meditator, healer,
this green Galena?

The false masculine considerations, the sly maneuvering,
would not be proffered. The absurd diplomacies, the evasions,
the ignorance both feigned and real . . . all would be set aside.
Yet would the inhabitants of the town, the world, be capable of
accepting and assisting her? They might be even less capable of
comprehending her than they had the coarse, impatient Gracchus.
He was a curiosity but not terribly unfamiliar, for he was hardly
more dead than they were, as they went about in their semblance
of living.

Jeffrey munched thoughtfully on his nails. Just outside his
chambers' door, uncomfortably close, someone was demanding
a labyrinth. "Give us the labyrinth to walk while we wait!"

He was neglecting them and they were desperately tolerating

all manner of gambits. But it was too late now, *too late*. Were ever sadder words to speak than those?

Daughter, Mother, Companion, Presence, the Green Galena. He should not have dismissed her but yesterday had been too soon. Too soon! But of course it had not been too soon. He'd been temporalizing, he'd behaved as though he hadn't been prepared.

The door was rattling in its sockets. "Give us the labyrinth to walk! And don't try to pass off that seven-ring one, we want the full eleven paths with lunations!" There were screams and approving howls. They had cleared the courtroom of themselves and were at his very threshold.

He allowed himself a chuckle. Of course they wanted their paths supersized, as geometrically concise as the labyrinth at Chartres which his tata had once seen and said that the experience had knocked any budding sense of the numinous right out of him. The thing was littered with folding chairs for the cathedral's innumerable interminable services and the only time you could see it the way it was supposed to be seen was just after it was mopped.

Jeffrey placed his mouth close to the door and suggested softly to the keening mob that they draw the labyrinth on the palm of their hands and finger-walk it. This seemed to mollify them somewhat and they quieted. "I'll be with you soon," he whispered.

Outside, massive lights were triggered, splashing his chambers with glare. Each dusk they made it official that night was no longer permitted. Erebus be gone! The owls lay fuddled and miserably starving in their hollows—their home, darkness had been taken from them. The very earth had been pressed to chalk, to clay, as through a mangle. The wolves, the bears, the great fish (which he had never seen) gone, even the harmless snakes and frogs of his childhood. If someone claimed he'd seen an eagle, he would not be taken seriously. The possibility of seeing an angel or a witch on a broomstick would be treated with more polite agnosticism. The fouling of the nest was all but complete, the birthright smashed.

He detested this most recent display of technological supremacy. Bouncing back from such historical earth-caused losses, humankind had become more frightened and ruthless than ever. Nature had been deemed sociopathic and if you found this position debatable you were deemed sociopathic as well and there were novel and increasingly effective ways of dealing with you. Half the fribbles who ended up in his courtroom had some need to atone, however stunted and unacknowledged. The other half believed they could still negotiate an outcome acceptable to them. It was discouraging. But discouragement was inadmissible . . . he would not be discouraged. He would be the destrier, charging through the icey towering waves of doubt and despair. But he was anxious, he had to admit, for hers would be a test case, his first. His first and last, for after this finding, there'd be no need for further precedents. He'd been fooling around up until now. It had all been childish stuff. He'd listened to them patiently for the most part. He had! But nothing was interested in them anymore, didn't they get it . . . Perhaps once but no longer.

Jeffrey—Enoch—swirled his robes around him. In a moment he'd venture a peek into his courtroom. He hoped they'd all be seated and staring at their hands as though they'd never noticed them before, dazed, but not suspicious. For woe if they suspected that they were no more than prisoners, with no place on earth to nurture them now and only the space they momentarily occupied to call their own.

I passed through the crowded court where people's heads were bowed in perplexed study and approached the bench but the chair on its swiveled wheels was empty. There was a flutter to my right and I saw a small smudged eye addressing me behind a slightly opened door. The door opened further and Jeffrey's pale gnawed hand beckoned.

We went up a few steps to his chambers, which was snug as a ship's cabin.

"I was concerned when I looked out and didn't see you," he said. "Are you familiar with the tree?"

"It's beautiful," I said.

"Yes yes, you're at a loss for words. Quite understandable," he said happily. "Where were we, where were we . . ."

"We were discussing the story about Gracchus. The fragment."

He smiled, his teeth white as a young dog's. "I thought we might compose something more," he said. "Less of a fragment. It could be within the parameters of what came before, though parameters are an arbitrary constant at best. The names will be different, the sexes will be less determined, standing of beings altered, appearances changed, the conversations, the methods of understanding, the inquiries most certainly, the dilemma posed."

"Another fiction," I said.

"It need not be fiction," he assured me. "And words might very well not suffice. They seldom have. The names which have been given to worldly things are the occasion of great error. Let's not speak of them. They have led us astray."

He turned and the robes spun around him in dark tortrix. "That's a nice sound, isn't it."

I closed my eyes. I recognized it but could not remember it, having never heard that sound of hundreds of beating wings, not even with my father as he rowed from our larger vessel and its anchorage far from shore. Silently he had rowed with us beside him on the thwart, looking upward into what had once been the great migration flyways.

In the captivating depths of the child judge's robes, I saw figures from my infancy, pondering me, not knowing my name, a window at twilight, the whorls of glass partitioned into nines above and below the sash, the world beyond to receive me and make its demands with semblances. I saw my mother and father

as two piers and myself the slip between them, a berth prepared. Then all drifted away, dissolving, and the figure, too, that I had thought myself to be.

"Words," he said, "have enabled us to get no nearer to . . ." He trailed off. "As an instance, the law . . ." He sighed and turned again, the robes gyring around him, creating the same wondrous sound of enraptured life in passage, an inhuman sound.

There was a violent crack as of a great breaking.

No dawn would reveal that the tree had been removed, trunk and branches, stump and roots. The rumored pages of books deep within the earth would not allow themselves to be recovered, though the sexton beetles and their consumption of all things dead, even dead words, might have devoured them over time. Human or animal remains would not be found as is occasionally the case when such an operation is executed.

"The court finds . . ." Jeffrey began.

But his heart wasn't in it. He blinked in the roaring, engulfing dark. Enoch and Galena, he thought without saying. That would have been a pairing. That would have been ideal.

A Note About the Author

Joy Williams is the author of four previous novels—including *The Quick and the Dead*, a finalist for the Pulitzer Prize—and five collections of stories, as well as *Ill Nature*, a book of essays that was a finalist for the National Book Critics Circle Award. Among her many honors are the Rea Award for the Short Story, the *Paris Review*'s Hadada Award and the Strauss Living Award from the American Academy of Arts and Letters. She was elected to the Academy in 2008.

A Note on the Type

This book was set in Fournier, a typeface named for Pierre Simon Fournier *le jeune* (1712–1768), a celebrated French type designer. Coming from a family of typefounders, Fournier was an extraordinarily prolific designer of typefaces and of typographic ornaments. He was also the author of the important *Manuel typographique* (1764–1766), in which he attempted to work out a system standardizing type measurement in points, a system that is still in use internationally.

*Typeset by North Market Street Graphics,*
*Lancaster, Pennsylvania*

*Printed and bound by Berryville Graphics,*
*Berryville, Virginia*

*Designed by Betty Lew*